OLD SOLDIER

OLD SOLDIER

A NOVEL

BY

Vance Bourjaily

DONALD I. FINE, INC.
New York

Library of Congress Cataloging-in-Publication Data
Bourjaily, Vance Nye.
Old soldier / Vance Bourjaily.
p. cm.
ISBN 1-55611-198-3
I. Title.
PS3503.07704   1990
813'.54--dc20   90-55334
                                                      CIP
Manufactured in the United States of America
Designed by Irving Perkins Associates

10 9 8 7 6 5 4 3 2 1

*For Inspector
A.N. Mogul,
Bombay Police,
Retired*

I

1

JOE MCKAY got what he wanted for his sixtieth birthday in April, a request for a divorce from the lady he had dumbass married five years earlier. Dingleberry Joe.

He hadn't known how much he wanted the gift until he made Deedee unwrap it, the evening of the birthday, in the calm that followed a fight wild enough to have blown out all the candles on the cake. If there'd been candles. Along with the divorce request came out the name of Deedee's new husband-elect, a Venezuelan who'd just bought the modelling school in New Haven in which Deedee McKay was head instructor.

This gentleman's name was either Hernandez or Fernandez, but could it be Gonzalez? He was speedy for a fact, and Joe was sure the surname had a *z* in it somewhere. Speedy Alzheimer.

Joe'd been in a wonderful mood ever since, with only a lapse now and then.

2

ONE OF these lapses took place in May, in a fancy electronics store, in a shopping center outside of Boston. Joe was on his way to fish for landlocked salmon in northern Maine. He walked into the joint grinning to buy the best damn battery-operated radio they had.

The clerk was a young black guy in a three-piece suit, who seemed to be in pretty fine fettle himself today. The clerk was also around seven inches taller than Joe, who stood a solid six-foot-one.

"Battery set, okay, okay," this tall clerk said. "Yes, I've got it here. Course, you can plug it in, too, but you're going where there's no electric?"

"Not one little kilowatt," Joe told him.

An elaborate piece of high-tech equipment in a metal case appeared in the counter, all gleaming dials, shiny knobs and fabric-covered speakers.

"Here's AM, FM, shortwave, computer tuning, and stereo cassette for ghetto-blasting, with all these levels here, Dolby . . . hey. Would you be wanting this to hear the semifinals?"

"Bullseye," Joe said. "The radio in my pickup's real nice if you enjoy listening to chain saws."

"I better warn you, this one's gonna groan if the Celts fall back."

"I'll groan with it," said Joe McKay. The Boston Celtics were a lost squad of walking wounded. The Milwaukee Bucks were fresh, dug-in and loaded.

The clerk and Joe went through a minute waltz of bragging and belittling, the ritual pleasure of seller and buyer. Joe had a credit card in his hand before it started. He played it like a glossy, plastic ace.

The clerk slapped it into a printer and ran it through. The clerk was so tall he looked comical, bending down to use the gadget. "Now tell me our Celts can make it," he said, looking up.

"You seem like you might know a whole lot more about it than me, short man."

The clerk straightened, stretched, and halfway pantomimed a hook shot. "Had a tryout with the Celts, the year I graduated P.C.U."

"What year?" P.C.U. was in Connecticut, not far from where Joe lived. Good basketball school.

"Year we made the final four." The clerk caught a high pass, drove a step and laid it up.

"Saw you on TV, but I'm not much on names."

"Barry Justin."

Joe shook his head, smiling. "What about your tryout?"

"You know what? My feet are too small. I can jump, but not like those guys."

"I've got size twelves, but it was all I could do to touch the rim." It was Joe's turn to get the phantom ball, indicate a pivot with his shoulders.

"Where'd you play?" Barry Justin's hand went out to stop Joe's shot.

"Just in the army, hey come on. You weren't born in time to block this ball." Barry stopped playing defense so Joe could can it. "We're some pair of jumpers. What about the Celts now?"

"They're playing old and tired."

"What's wrong with the bench this year?"

"Kacey doesn't give the young guys playing time. They can't get into game rhythm. Here." Gave Joe the credit card slip to sign, put the card itself into the device which would transmit approval. "You'll be able to hear them breathe on this set."

"I hope they still got five guys breathing," Joe said, happily signing for $279. "You married, jumper?" He got his card back, put it away, and pulled the radio towards himself.

"No, no. Not me."

"When you're married, you negotiate at home for a week before you buy something like this. Then you go to a discount store, where the stuff's still in boxes, but you're not looking at merchandise anyway. You're looking at price tags. Show me how to play a casette, and I'm on my way."

"Let me get a cassette."

"Right here in my pocket." Joe got it out of the breast pocket of his blue wool-flannel shirt, and handed it over.

The tall clerk turned on the set, adjusted a couple of things, and slid Joe's tape into the right slot. There was a click, a hum, the sound of drones, and a shrill, discordant, sawing wail. Goddamn thrilling.

"Something's wrong." Alarmed, the clerk pressed *reject*, and stopped the sound.

"No. It's fine. Play the thing."

"What is it?"

"Solo bagpipe," Joe said. "As a matter of fact, it's my brother playing."

"Yeah? Hey, I should have known. I heard that before, but it was a band."

"Band?"

"Between halves. We were playing a tournament out at Iowa." He started the music again, more softly. "That was weird, hearing it in a place like that. They had this girls' bagpipe pep band . . ."

"This week my brother's been in Nova Scotia . . ." Joe said that much, stopped, and pushed *reject* himself. "Balls. Girls' bagpipe pep band."

"Excuse me?"

"It's okay."

"No, what's the matter, man? The set?"

"This younger brother of mine was in a kind of bag-pipe pep band. Kids. Back home in Glasgow, Kentucky. The Glaswegian Kilts. Nevermind." He got the radio under his arm. "Thanks, jumper."

During the birthday battle, Deedee had smashed a forty-year-old framed photograph of Joe's brother, Tommy, as a blond boy in his parade kilt. She'd driven a shard into the kid's handsome face, laughed like a maniac when she saw it, and shrieked:

"The big fat faggot's got a hole in his head."

3

WHEN JOE came out of the store, into the shopping center parking lot, there was a very young Pfc. in fatigues and cap, carrying a musette bag and looking over Joe's rig, which resembled a comic strip, two-car freight train. The locomotive was a big, red, 4-wheel-drive Chevy pickup with a black camper top, all fresh-waxed, and with a bashed-up aluminum canoe strapped to the roof, proud of its scars. The caboose was a fifteen-year-old, pop-up camper, a little lopsided, but scrubbed up clean the day before.

"Morning," Joe said to the GI. "How's it going?" Joe

knew he was about to be asked for a ride. He wasn't sure how he felt about company. He had things to think about. And he had bagpipe music in his ears, and wanted to play the rest of Tommy's tape.

"Mister, are you going East?" Up here they said *East* when they meant North.

"How'd you know?"

"You got those Connecticut plates, and that canoe."

"So I do."

"Figured you could be on your way fishing, if you ain't already coming back."

"Going," Joe said, and what the hell. "You need a lift?"

"Ayah. Got to get to Bangor, Maine."

"I'm going up past Bangor," Joe said. "Get in, if you don't mind hearing some music you might not care for."

"I like music." The boy held out his hand. He was wiry and freckled, with blond hair and a strong right hand. "Name's David Roy."

"I'm Joe McKay. But maybe not this music. Let me have your musette, David."

Joe took the bag, set the radio down carefully, and straddled the trailer hitch. He squeezed back against the front of the pop-up to open the rear window of the camper top. His gear was stowed under it on the truck bed quite precisely: two cased fly-rods lined up, new waders folded beside them, new wading shoes still in the box, revarnished canoe paddles, duffel bag squared away, fishing vest folded, gas can forward, and a small outboard hanging upright, just behind the can. There was a sheet-metal smoker he'd made a long time ago that still worked fine, tied up parallel to the motor. What the hell was he doing? Passing inspection?

Then it was the new wading shoes to which Joe's gaze

returned, and fondly. He'd never felt he ought to spring for the felt-soled kind before the divorce, and couldn't have afforded forty-eight bucks for a pair before the marriage. Joe liked good equipment and liked taking care of it, but it was kind of stupid that something like a pair of wading shoes could bring back the sense of well-being he'd lost for a dark moment inside the store.

What was nice was having a little disposable money, and feeling free to dispose of it as he liked.

Rearranging things slightly, wondering if he was getting past neat and into fussy, he stowed his guest's musette bag square in the chosen place, closed up, unstraddled, went around and unlocked the right-hand door.

"Climb in," he said.

Pfc. David Roy didn't climb. He leapt, as if he thought Joe might take back the offer if the rider wasn't quick about it.

"Looks like you really want to get to Bangor," Joe said.

"I got to." That was as much as Pfc. Roy seemed to have to say on the subject as they started off.

As soon as they were on the Interstate, Joe got out the bagpipe cassette from his shirt pocket again.

"David," he said. "I need to listen to this. If it sounds too godawful to you, just say so. I could play it later, after you get off."

This was apparently alarming enough to fetch David out of some kind of trance. "Why? What is it?"

"Bagpipe music. I was raised with it."

"You Scotch?"

"Kentucky Scotch. My old man was a piper. I used to fool with it, but this tape is my brother, Tommy. He's one of the best."

"He make his living doing that?"

"No, he plays fiddle in a New York country-music bar. But he likes to enter bagpipe contests." Joe heard himself getting garrulous, as sometimes seemed to happen, now that he was living alone again. In marriage you got used to saying your junk thoughts out loud, the other person hearing but not listening, the other person ready any time to start cranking out her own stuff in the pauses. "He's playing in a contest in Canada this last week."

"How'd he make out?"

"I'll know tomorrow, up on the Pemberton. Tommy's going to join me."

"Used to go fishing with my brother, 'fore the Army."

Joe tried to think whether he and Tommy had ever gone fishing together, and decided they probably hadn't. By the time Tommy was fishing age, Joe was already in the army. Maybe Tom would have turned out different if he'd had a big brother at home. One of Joe's most troubling memories, the one that had recurred again in the store, was of being nineteen, home on leave from the big war, and going to a Scottish Games picnic where the Glaswegian Kilts were playing and being introduced. Standing in the crowd, Joe heard a man say, "I hear that pretty blond one sucks a sweet dick."

Joe had whirled, looking for the guy to hit, thought he saw who it was, but couldn't get to him. Joe had to get older before he learned to live with Tommy's being gay. Joe had had to serve with homosexual guys in the wars, and learn that some of them could soldier, to get his head straight about the matter. What he now said to David Roy was,

"No. Tommy's not a fisherman. He's probably a guy

who needs some rest," and started the tape on the new machine which was between them on the seat.

The first tune was a march, "Balmoral Highlanders." It was simple enough so that Joe had once been able to play it himself. He didn't know if Pfc. Roy was paying much attention, and was a little surprised to hear the kid say, as the march ended:

"Ayah, that fires you up, don't it?"

Joe stopped the tape for a moment. "It's supposed to. Couple of hundred years ago, when the British were breaking up the power of the clans, they made the bagpipes illegal. They hung a guy, James Reid, for carrying a bagpipe. Said it was an instrument of war. How's that for disarmament?"

Pfc. Roy didn't seem to want to comment on how that was for disarmament, but he didn't seem to mind the music, either. Joe started it up again, and, after a couple more tunes, the rider wanted to know what a *strathspey* was, reading the word from the casette cover.

"It's a slow dance. I forget which one we've got."

" 'Arniston Castle'."

Joe played it. David said it was pretty. He was getting into reading the titles.

" 'The Braes of Locheil'. Is that how you say it?"

"Close enough. It's one my dad played. It's slow, too, about wanting to go home, to where the deer are. I could play it once myself."

"Like 'Home on the Range'?"

"Yes. Like that." Whatever was waiting for David Roy in Bangor, he was hearing Tommy McKay's music now and thinking about it.

"Play it again. You want to?" David said.

"Maybe later. We're ready for the pibroch now. Let me tell you what it means."

The pibrochs, Joe told him, were the finest things in bagpipe music, far longer and more difficult to play than reels and jigs and marches, a different kind of music, really, and the kind the purists really loved. Joe McKay, dingleberry teacher. Pibrochs were tough for a listener, too, because of their length and complication, like those classical pieces for solo violin or cello.

"Sonatas?" Asked Dingleberry Roy, and then apologized. "My mom's a piano teacher."

Sure. No harm in that. As Joe was saying: this pibroch, "Lament for the Children," would take fifteen minutes. Like a lot of the others, it had a legend that went with it, and as often happened, the legend was about the Mac-Crimmons.

For seven generations and three hundred years, the MacCrimmons were hereditary pipers to the Clan McLeod. The MacCrimmons were the greatest who ever played, who ever composed, who ever taught. Pipers from other clans, legend said, were sent to the Isle of Skye to study with the MacCrimmons, and the training took seven years.

Joe glanced at David Roy, and had him by the ears. Patric Mor MacCrimmon, some books said, went to church one Sunday in 1610, accompanied by eight strong sons. Before the year was over, seven of the boys were dead of the plague.

Now there are four kinds of pibrochs, Joe said, driving on the almost-empty Interstate: gatherings, to call a clan to war; battles, to fire the fighters up; salutes, to celebrate; and laments, to mourn. When his seven sons were

dead, Patrick Mor wrote this one, *Cumha na Cloinne,*
"Lament for the Children."

"You ready?"

"Play it," David said.

But then another book thought maybe it went back to
the sixth century, the days of Old King Cole, King Conol
of Cantyre, who lost his son, Mhuil Duin. And another
book, according to Tommy, said it was the deaths by
drowning of three girls, two of them Campbells, the
other Joe couldn't remember.

"Please play it," David said. "I think it was them seven
boys."

"Lament for the Children" started with the drones,
and then the chanter striking a note that was almost
pretty. Then the ground began, three harsh, middle-reg-
ister cries, and then ascent to a high note of great purity,
the cries again, the descent to a pure low, held like a
pause.

"It's like an animal crying," David Roy said. "That's
almost smart enough to talk."

If you like, Joe thought, listening. But it's a man outdoors and solitary, in the mountains. By the water. With
a grief for which he has no words, letting it elaborate
itself in long, slow pulses . . . "Lament for the Children"
started slow and never gained speed, the same progress
from harsh to pure repeated, grace notes added in the
variations, but never busily, always with a grave, heart-
broken dignity. Roy had stopped talking, Joe had
stopped thinking, when the great pibroch ended with a
final, abrupt cry. The tape was done. The throb of the
pipes faded into cool air.

After a moment David Roy said: "The seven sons, or

the three girls. Old King Cole's boy . . . but what I kept seeing was them kids on the milk cartons, you know? All the missing children. 'Have you seen me'?"

Joe nodded. "That pibroch has all the tears in it a brave man could ever allow himself to cry."

"Can we hear it again?"

"Sure. Pretty soon. What's your problem, son?"

"Who says I got a problem?"

"You're AWOL, aren't you?"

"Why do you say?"

"Fellow on pass doesn't travel in fatigues."

"I better get out right here," David said.

"If you want to. Or I can stop asking."

"How about that one about the deer? Will you play that?"

"Sure." It took a little fiddling with the tape before Joe found "The Braes of Locheil" again, and let it run through. "Okay. Take a nap or something. We'll stop for a hamburger. Then we'll do the 'Lament' again."

"It's my sister," David Roy said.

"I apologize for asking, kid. You don't have to pay for the ride with a story."

"Her husband beat her up bad."

"In Bangor?"

"Ayah. Ain't the first time, but I guess it's the worst. The fucking asshole . . ."

"How bad? If you want to tell me."

"Hospital bad. And of course she won't call the cops."

"How'd you find out?"

"Mom called. They sent for me to come to the orderly room for a call, and she told me. So I just, just hit the road."

"You walked out of the orderly room, grabbed your kit, and kept going, just like that?"

"Yessir."

"Who was there?"

"Sir?"

"In the orderly room?"

"Company clerk. Jerry."

"Did you tell Jerry?"

"No, sir. I did not."

"Tell anyone?"

"Something like this, about my family?"

"David." Joe said it in a way so preemptory he surprised himself. He pulled off onto the disabled lane, stopped the truck, and had to know one more thing before he got started on this soldier. "What do you aim to do when you get to Bangor?"

"I'm going to hunt the asshole down. He used a stick on on her. He's going to learn all about getting beat up, and I won't need no stick. How come you stopped?"

"Can you handle this guy?"

"He's a little bigger, but he ain't got the balls to fight men. Just women. And he's got a beer belly . . ." David's right fist was clenched in his left palm.

"All right, soldier."

"You going to tell me not to do it?"

"Hell, no. Go after him. There's things we don't call cops for when we can take care of them ourselves. But why in the name of pisscat alley are you trying to fuck yourself up?"

"Sir?"

"Don't you have any goddamn sense at all?" David Roy looked stunned. "You're probably a pretty fair young

soldier, when you're not being a stupid piece of arma-
dillo shit. Sit up, will you? I don't believe you've got
enough sense to beat a beer belly."

"What'd I do to you, Mr. McKay?"

"To me? To yourself, stink brain. What do you want to
do? Lose your stripe?"

"Screw the stripe."

"Go to the stockade? Look out through the bars, mon-
keyface. That's really going to help sis, isn't it, when the
beer belly knows you're locked away and starts looking
for a bigger stick." There was a pause, and Joe softened
his voice. "Why couldn't you take time to take this to
your company commander, Roy? Or your first sergeant?"

"Something like this, about my family?"

"You don't think they'd help you out?"

"You don't know First Sergeant Hardwick. He's on
everybody's ass, and I mean all day long."

"I hope the hell he is. That's his job. Who else is going
to keep you little peckeronies salty?" Joe yelled it, hardly
understanding how he'd got so angry. "You know what
else his job is? Taking care of you sparrow farts, goddamn it. Who makes sure you get your pay? Your food?
Your mail? Who's on the ass of the mess sergeant? The
clerk? Supply sergeant? Mail orderly? And I mean all day
long. But you wouldn't go to him when you needed him.
You think hardass Hardwick wouldn't have given you a
damn pass? And fixed it up with the old man? What the
hell do you think it's all about, soldier?"

"That's what you were," David Roy said, a hand on the
door latch. "A damn first sergeant."

"Twenty-six years," Joe McKay said. "And three wars.

And if one of my feeny-peenies had business like you've got and didn't bring it to me, just walked off? I'd have taken off my stripes when he came back, and personally knocked his ass up and down the parade ground, left ball, right ball, for company punishment. Before I told the clerk to write up the court martial."

Roy yelled back. "It's personal. It ain't the goddamn army's business."

"Keep it up, stupid. Where is this outfit of yours?"

"What would I want to tell you for?"

"Keep it up. Get stupider."

"New Jersey. I'm in tanks."

"You got that orderly room phone number?"

"You want to turn me in, fuck off, sergeant. I'll do what I gotta do."

"You got two choices. We're going down the next exit. You can give me that damn phone number, or you can get yourself another ride."

Roy hesitated. Then he said, "It's in my musette bag. I got an address book. What are you gonna do, Top?"

"You gonna trust me?"

"I got to, Top. I gotta get to Bangor."

4

THERE WAS a pay phone at the 7-Eleven. Joe told Pfc. Roy to gas up the truck while Joe made his call. First Sergeant McKay, Company M, 2nd Battallion, 24th Infantry, calling First Sergeant Hardwick.

Hardwick came on the line and said, "Yeah Sergeant. Your outfit stationed here, or what?"

"Far as I know, my outfit deactivated long ago. Me too. Retired in '68."

"Fucking congratulations. What the hell are you selling?"

"I got one of your ding dongs riding in my truck," Joe said. "AWOL. On his way to Bangor, Maine."

"Fucking David Roy. Wring his chicken neck for me, will you? That little cunt sniffer's supposed to be driving . . . What the hell do you want to turn the kid in for, McKay?"

"Like him, do you?"

"Up to today, he was next man to make corporal. Today he is one freckle-prick deserter, and I'm putting out an all-points with the Maine state cops . . . what the hell is it, Top? Kid got family problems?"

Joe told him.

"Goddamn," Sergeant Hardwick said. "Okay. Goddamit. You believe him?"

"Yeah. He's a pretty sincere type of a ding dong."

"What do you want me to do?"

"Mail him a pass," Joe said. "You've got his home address?"

"I'll mail him his ass on a platter," Hardwick said. "Yeah. We got the address."

"Thanks, Top."

"Hey, McKay. Tell the little fart to give the asshole a couple of shots for me, will you? And make it stick. He's on parade here Monday morning, or he's up to his baby blues in brown."

Joe said thanks again, and hung up. Pfc. Roy was looking at him, the gas hose still sticking in the fill-hole.

"You'll get your pass in the mail," Joe said. "Let's move
out."

5

ONCE HE'D discharged David Roy, Joe lapsed again,
thinking he might have been more patient with Deedee
in the last couple of years. She could be sweet and fun,
when she wasn't exercising her talent as a world-class
nag.

She was a tall, reckless, forty-three-year-old blonde,
with a slim, seductive figure and an American-girl, bob-
nose face. She'd been a model once, and then a Pan-
American stewardess. Used that connection to take them
on a rambunctious, steak-eating honeymoon to Argen-
tina.

They'd learned golf together first year of the marriage.
Joe had the power, naturally, but Deedee's game had
more finesse so they were pretty equal. She was very
good on the greens, and he laughed, remembering a cool
day, when they seemed to have the links to themselves.
Deedee sank a really long putt, and when Joe knelt down
to get her ball out of the cup, she came running at him,
crying,

"Did you see that? Did you see that, you big ape?"
Pushed him over, laughing and kissing, rolled him on

top of her, hiked up her skirt and they were off, right on the green of the eighth hole, 271 yards, par 4.

She'd got him to take her up to the Laurentians for a week, their first winter, and taught him to ski, which he loved in a clumsy way, and at which she was absolutely beautiful. They made the skiing trip every year. This year they'd gone in February, but had a stupid running fight which spoiled two days of it. It started because she wanted to dress up for dinner, and Joe said,

"Hell, I've got a good-looking sweater. So have you. What's wrong with that?" He'd been grouchy, he guessed, because there were a lot of good-looking young single guys staying at the lodge. Didn't say so, but figured Deedee wanted the fine gentlemen to find her attractive. He was seventeen years older.

See that camper in the rearview mirror? That one there. For some reason, Deedee adored getting laid in it. God, the way she'd run a fingernail up and down his spine, through the shirt, and whisper, breathing into his ear.

"Hey, lover. Want to pop it up?" Look out, ear.

They'd liked cooking together at first. Then they had to agree that they did get into one another's way, so they took turns if they weren't going out. They were pretty busy people and ate out a lot. And liked to give small parties, there were half a dozen couples in town they had fun with. But they hadn't thrown any parties in a while, and the last one they were invited to, Bill and Tacy's, Deedee didn't want to go, got deeply pissed when Joe said maybe he'd go alone, and then all of a sudden turned into a perfect doll about it, and said sorry, let's do go, and they'd gone. And she'd flirted so hard with Bill that Bill got embarrassed about it, so Joe put his hand very publicly and very crudely on Tacy's very pretty ass, and they all laughed, he'd made his point, defused the situation, and collected his reward in bed when they got home, real, real good . . . and that was the last time, come to think of it . . . She was the only woman he wanted during the time of their marriage.

Well, she was gone. As the limey's liked to say, what you gain on the swings, you lose on the roundabouts, but that sixtieth birthday party had been a real, red rubber, ringdangdoo.

It started about forty-five minutes after Joe got home from work at the truck stop he managed, and of which he owned a little piece. He was carrying what was left of a chocolate cake the truck-stop waitresses had bought him, most of which they'd managed to eat up themselves, once Joe started cutting it.

He parked his pickup in front of the Cape Cod cottage he and Deedee were buying, on a pretty residential street in Tillbury, twenty miles north of New Haven, and ten east of Joe's place of business. There was an early moon in the Connecticut sky, and clouds moving across it.

Spring, when you lived near the river, was when the lid came off the gray box you'd been living in all winter, and you could see the sky again. Shook loose all sorts of shit in people, animals and birds. Insects. Viruses. Come on.

He saw that Deedee's Porsche wasn't in the driveway, checked and learned that it wasn't shut up in the garage, either, and so much for the martini and blow job Joe'd expected her to greet him with. It wasn't that he'd wanted these items especially, any more than he'd wanted to help eat the big chocolate cake. He generally drank bourbon these days, wasn't notably horny this evening, and seldom ate sweets. But a guy had to go along with the people who liked observing his occasions with him. Deedee, having surprised him with the martini-plus ritual the first birthday after they'd got married, had proferred it three times since, and Joe'd reciprocated on her birthday, except that the booze of choice was French champagne.

So it was odd walking into a dark house, and the first thing he did when the lights were on was phone the modelling school to see if Deedee was working late. No answer.

The second thing he did was mix a bourbon and water.

There was evidence of a minor shopping frenzy in the kitchen. Deedee seemed to have made it to the wholesale club and back before work, which didn't begin until eleven. There were cases of canned V-8 juice, hearts of palm and tuna; there was a box of 144 garbage bags, a bale of paper towels, a new toaster oven, many panty hose, huge plastic bottles of shampoo and conditioner— which probably triggered the trip; she was low on shampoo—and, goddamit, a carton of the hard-finished, single-ply toilet paper the wholesale club dealt in. He'd asked her to stop buying the wretched stuff several times. She probably didn't save a nickel a roll on it, but Deedee was one of those shoppers—pay premium price for the big ticket items like rhino and elephant turds, and try to make up for it by econo-mizing on mouse shit.

In her fifteen Pan-Am stewardess years, Joe imagined, there must have been bazaars all over the world that closed to celebrate the day after her crew left town.

He finished his first drink, put away the wholesale
club stuff that went in the kitchen, and sat down with his
second drink and the evening paper. He was reading
about a golf tournament, in which Gary Player was lead-
ing the field, when headlights lit up the driveway outside
the kitchen window for a moment, and then went out.
Joe unlocked the kitchen door and opened it. Deedee
came in shivering.

"God," she said. "It's cold out there. Can you turn up
the heat?" She was wearing a polo coat he liked to see her
in, but it didn't seem to have kept her warm enough.

Joe closed the door, turned her way and grinned.
"Sure. Happy birthday."

Her hands went straight to her crotch. She looked
funny, awkward, and somehow endearing, holding onto
herself that way. "I forgot. I forgot."

Joe laughed. "It's all right," he said. "You can turn
yourself loose. It's something I wouldn't mind forgetting
myself."

"But you're sixty."

Pee-culiar. She didn't run over to hug him. Instead she
took the polo coat off and draped it on a chair. Piss-
culiar. "Want a drink? I thought we'd go out to dinner."

"Some wine?" She gestured toward the fridge. "Did
you remember to buy white wine?"

"Didn't you?" He indicated the rest of the crap from
the wholesale club, which he hadn't got around to taking
upstairs. They generally bought their bottles at the club.

"Oh no. You're the one who knows all about wine,
aren't you?"

"Come on . . ."

"You always have to buy the wine, excuse me, select

the wine, don't you? I flew all over the world for fifteen years, serving wine to passengers from every country, talking to them about wine. Learning about it. Taking classes. But you're the big shit wine man, you're the one who knows . . ."

During this Joe strolled over to the fridge and opened it. "There's Dubonnet. Want it?"

"For your information, big shit, Dubonnet is not white wine. You hear? They're different things."

"It's got a wine base, for Christ's sake. You want some or not?"

"You tried to tell me it was white wine." But she held out a glass for him to pour into, and drank off the Dubonnet in one pull. It put him in mind of a certain mountain girl with a shot glass of shine. Deedee held out her glass for more. So had the mountain girl.

"Good stuff?" Joe wanted to soften the mood.

"It's not white wine."

"You made that point." He was starting to feel irritated. He kicked the carton of toilet paper, hard enough to move it smartly across the kitchen floor for a couple of yards. "I've asked you to stop buying this junk, haven't I?"

"It's a good buy. Now that you know all about wine, you can start learning about toilet paper. Or did you think we were made of money?" She took a stand in front of the carton, as if to protect it from him. "It's a very good buy."

"It's very bad toilet paper."

"I like it."

"Oh in that case, I mean if you really have nice times with it . . ."

"Oh, shut up."

Joe laughed. "Do I get a kiss or not?"

"You get a kick in the balls if you make any more of your crude jokes. A person can get pretty sick of your idea of humor."

"I suppose."

"I shop very carefully to keep this household solvent. I took time out of a very busy morning to get things we need. But you, you can't even take time to put them away. I thought you were supposed to be Mr. Neat and Orderly. Why haven't you put things away instead of sitting there, drinking and reading the paper?"

"Sure."

"And you want me to go out of my way to buy gourmet toilet paper."

He couldn't help it. He started laughing again.

"What are you laughing about, macho prick?"

He pointed at the gallon jug of shampoo. "You got plenty of sauce for the toilet paper, didn't you?"

"My shampoo." She swept the big plastic bottle up and into her arms.

"Why did you get so damn much of it? You'll switch to some other brand before you use a quarter of that."

"You stay away from this shampoo. I couldn't wash my hair this morning, thanks to you using up all the shampoo."

"Bullshit," Joe said. "I left plenty."

"You didn't leave enough to wash a mouse."

"Oh, come on, Deedee."

"Come on? Here come on . . ." And she threw the shampoo bottle to him so suddenly he was barely able to catch it. "Take my lipstick, too. Take my makeup. Go ahead. That's what my job's about, looking good, but you don't give a shit."

"Deedee, what in hell's the matter?"

"Give me that." Now she wanted the jug back again. "Inconsiderate, jerk-off bastard. Never think of anybody but yourself."

"Is that right?"

"Yourself and your faggot brother."

"What the hell's Tommy got to do with it?"

"I hate him. You and he can kiss my royal ass together."

"Delightful invitation."

She hugged the bottle tighter, and the scream she'd been working up to came out.

"All right. That's enough," Joe shouted. "I'm sorry I used up your shampoo, but that's not enough to make you cut off your teats and stomp them."

She dropped the plastic bottle and came at him, screaming and beating him on the chest. "You think everythings a joke."

"I think you could ruin a good pair of shoes that way, stupid. And what the hell does Tommy have to do with it, I asked you?"

With Deedee and Tommy it had been disgust at first sight. She gave Joe a last whack with both hands, ran out of the kitchen and came storming back, holding the framed portrait of Tommy as a kid in his kilt. "This bastard." She shook the photo at Joe. "I wish I had him just like this. He tried to call me at work today, that's what." And she yelled, "I was busy on another line, you hear?"

"Why would he want to call you?"

"So he talked to Victor."

"Who the hell is Victor?"

"I hate him talking to Victor. The faggot teased Victor."

"Teased Victor."

"About his accent, that cocksucker. At least Victor doesn't talk with a mouth full of cornpone, like you shitty little Southern boys."

"It was probably something about my birthday." Now Joe was yelling, too. "But of course you couldn't be bothered to call him back."

"No, I didn't call the big, fat faggot back," she said, and slammed the picture against the doorknob, shattering the glass. "There." She looked at it, and burst into hysterical laughter. "See that? Oh, see the pretty face."

The shard of glass had Tommy right between the eyes.

"All right," Joe shouted, grabbing, from where it hung on the kitchen wall, a poster photo, made in her modelling days, of Deedee in a chief's hat. "Let's cook, chef." He turned on a burner on the gas stove, and passed the front of the poster through the flame to blister it. "Want it rare or fucking well-done?" He yelled, and she hurled the photo of Tommy at him.

Joe deflected it onto the floor, and scaled the poster toward the trash basket. "Let's fuck up some more pictures. Let's get your wonderful albums. Come on."

Deedee looked around, probably for something else to throw, saw Joe's open bottle of Jim Beam and side-swiped it onto the floor with the edge of her hand.

"Have a drink, pig." She stepped beside him and took his wrist. "Get on your hands and knees and have a drink, shitty alcoholic pig." And she actually tried to move him into the puddle.

Joe pulled away and went for the Dubonnet. "Let's

make it a cocktail." He started to pour the aperitif into the whiskey.

"Give me that." She came at him with her fingernails spread toward his face. Joe dropped the Dubonnet and caught her wrists.

"Will you tell me what the fuck's going on?"

"Let me go."

"Goddamit, where were you after work?"

There was one more scream from her, and a frantic yank, strong enough to pull her free. She stumbled backward, slipped in the puddle of booze, and went down on her right side. Her skirt went riding up her thigh, and Joe had a wild impulse to follow her into the acrid puddle, push the skirt all the way up and embrace her. He was even half-erected, and he went down on one knee and reached out to her. She rolled away and started to cry. "You hit me."

Joe stood, the impulse and the erection, the anger and the lust, all changing into weariness, with a touch of sorrow. "No. No, I didn't, Deedee. You slipped, baby."

He held out the hand again to help her up, but she sat up first before taking it, and said in a little-girl voice: "Yes. I know you wouldn't hit me, Joe. Harry used to hit me."

Harry was the pilot with whom she'd lived for years. She let Joe help her up, but then she backed away a couple of steps.

"What is the matter?"

"Nothing. Well, nothing."

"Come on. Where were you after work?"

"Well, with Victor."

"Where with Victor?"

"Yes."

"What does 'yes' mean?"

"In his apartment."

"You were laying him?"

She didn't say no, and there was something to fight about now, but the fight was over. He felt a fair amount of pain.

"Victor wants me to marry him."

"Marry him." He was getting ahold of the pain, squeezing it into a little plastic ball of don't-give-a-shit. "Yeah, you better do that."

"I'm sorry, Joe."

"You've known the man two weeks," Joe said. Then, curiously, as if she were no more to him than one of the waitresses who sometimes brought him their troubles: "You want to marry Victor?"

She nodded and said, in a tearful voice: "I want a divorce."

"Sure," Joe said, his odd moment of feeling distant from all this turning into even an odder moment when he felt on the brink of exhilaration. "Hey, you got your divorce."

"Joe?"

It was the prospect of a freedom he'd never considered seeking that began to excite him, but he didn't want her to see it. Or to know that the pain could come back, either. He powerfully wanted to get out of her presence.

"Joe, what are you going to do?"

"I'm going to get some dinner," he said, trying not to let himself feel anything more confusing right now than hungry.

Later, when he got back, he found she'd mopped up,

rinsed the liquor out of her dress and hung it in the
bathroom, packed a suitcase and left a note with Victor's
phone number. By now Joe's feelings were zooming,
flashing and going blank, like the night sky on the
Fourth of July.

It was strange to be alone again. He'd had a wife once
before, the mountain girl. She'd died in a theatre fire
when Joe was in Korea. After that he'd been shacked up
from time to time, but mostly it was Saturday night
women, when he could turn one up. Living alone became his habit until Deedee came along and knocked
him for a loop. So now he was going to stop looping,
after five years, and would have to learn straight and
level flight again.

He had a drink from a new bottle of Beam. He'd had
several drinks at the restaurant he'd gone to, along with
a steak he couldn't eat. He walked around, trying out this
alone-at-home business, liking it, having another drink,
feeling the pain rush back.

What he wanted was to talk to dumb old Tommy
about it, good and bad, but Tommy worked nights.

Then the phone rang, startling him. He let it ring twice
more, stiffening himself, getting set for Deedee, but,
think of the Devil, it was dumb old Tommy himself.

6

TOMMY MCKAY had tried to call his ridiculous brother several times during the day. He'd tried the merry old truck stop, where the office phone didn't answer, and the waitresses couldn't seem to handle taking messages. Then he'd thought of calling the detestable Deedee, to ask her to buy the sixty-year-old wild turkey a bottle of Wild Turkey on Tommy's behalf, and found himself talking to a remarkably thick-skulled Latino who insisted that if Tommy wanted to take modellink lesson, Tommy mus' calm to de skull for inderfew his personal self, it did not make different whose brudd-in-law.

How much dumb shit must a man endure? Tommy said, slowly and distinctly, that he vass brudd-in-law Khadafy, and vould one car bomb send to these modellink skull, salaam aleikum, and hung up.

Then the day got busier than a Burmese gang-bang and stayed that way until just now, 10:30 P.M., at the X-Bar Country and Western Club. The other dunces in the band were wiping brows and swiping booze when Tommy reached the manager's office where he went each night at break time to wash up and put on a fresh cowboy shirt. He buttoned it on, a soft, blue-and-tan plaid number, picked up the phone and dialed Joe's house.

"Hello?" Big brother sounded drunk.

"Joe McKay. You gonna take that sixty-year old foot out of the grave, or put the other one in?"

"Tommy. Goddamn, who I wanted to talk to."

"Happy birthday, big, drunk brother."

"Big yourself. What are you weighing in at these days? About two-ten?"

Joe's guess was about fifteen pounds light, but Tommy didn't see why a man should say so. "Close. Very close."

"Heard you'd been trying to get me," Joe said.

"Triple-D passed the word? How is the whore?"

"That's what I wanted to talk about. The whore is gone."

"Oh, no."

"Fuckin' A."

Tommy broke into his Billy Holiday falsetto. *So tell me/ How could it/ Be true?* Then he crowed like a rooster, "Ur-urur-ur-urrr. Look out, chickens." God this made him happy. "Please don't say you're upset about it."

"Like I'd busted through the fence, but I got a few wire cuts doing it," Joe said. "Otherwise, I mostly feel like another drink."

"Hop on the midnight special. Let's go after it."

"Midnight special don't run til mornin'," Joe said. "What's this about you teasin' Deedee's bossman? He's gonna marry up with her, yessir."

"Hopin' he's got looks and money, he sure was ahint the door when the brains was give out. You want to drive down?"

"Not the way I'm drinking. Japanese sandman's practicing karate chops."

So Tommy sang a few bars of that one, *Silver for gold/ New dreams for old,* seemed right on the money, softened his voice and said, "Sayonara, baby."

"Victor," Joe said. "Fernandez, by God."

"Huh?

"'Night. I better quit and call you tomorrow."

Joe hung up. So did Tommy, smiling, picked up his
fiddle, started back to the bandstand through the
crowded tables, and felt himself groped.

"Easy down there, podnah," he said, moving on, holding the fiddle high, and must a man look down to see
who the groper was? What the fuck for?

An epicene voice said, "Hey, Big Dog?" and another
said, "There goes the Dog."

7

NEXT MORNING when Jubilee Joseph called, Tommy was
sitting by the telephone in his favorite dressing gown, a
red-and-gold silk foulard which a dear boy had made for
him several years back. Tommy was doing two things he
enjoyed.

One was drinking cappuccino; a dear boy named Albert had just brewed and mixed it for Tommy on the
shiny $385 espresso machine, which Tommy had in-
cluded as a piece of living room furniture, because he
loved the way it looked. The other thing Tommy was
doing for pleasure was listening to the calls come in over
his answering machine, with the speaker on, the callers
having heard the tape saying Tommy wasn't available.

Albert, young with a silky mustache, in a velour jogging suit with his own cappuccino, was listening, too.

The phone would ring, the machine play a few bars of Tommy's theme song, "Stuttering Strings," followed by Tommy's recorded voice saying, "There's a b-natural beep coming your way soon. After that, it's your turn."

Over the speaker, just before Joe's call, a caller's voice had said: "This is Brendan from N'Awlins . . ."

"The Crescent City," Tommy explained to Albert.

"The Big Easy," Albert explained back. They had lived together in New Orleans once.

". . . And I'm a friend of Jamie Ponchatoula's?"

"Any friend of Jamie's?" Albert inquired.

"Probably slept in the street last night," Tommy said.

The voice said: "Jamie said call you about a place to stay."

"You see?" said Tommy.

"You didn't like our streets, Brendan?" Albert asked.

"Park Avenue and 65th's an excellent address," said Tommy, drowning out Brendan's report of his where-abouts and phone number, but it didn't matter. Tommy would play the call back later, return it and give the wooly weasel a couple of crash pad numbers on the old dear-boy network. Better, he'd have Albert make the call, tender the numbers, and explain that Tommy him-self was caught up in an absolutely exhausting rehearsal and recording schedule, which was the very plain Jane's clitoral truth.

In another minute there came another ring, the greet-ing, and after the b-natural, Joe's baritone voice saying: "Tommy. I'm at work. Try me here and I'll keep trying you."

Tommy grabbed the phone and pushed a button. "Hey now. I'm right here, playing telephone, Jojo."

"Playing what?"

"Listening to the beagles lined up to barf into my telephone, leaving their wonderful messages because they think I'm not home."

"You must be one popular little two-hundred-ten-pound pissant."

"Utterly so, Joe."

"Smartass."

"Just a humble country fiddle-player, lost in smartass city."

"Still at the X-Bar?"

"I'm the reason for the X-Bar."

"Nothing to do with the rest of the band."

"I'm the reason for them, too. You can't believe the work I'm getting those peons. Studio gigs, new album . . ." Albert signalling him about something. "Just a mo'. Joe. Hold it."

"Hold what? My dick?"

"If you can find it at your age." He covered the mouthpiece. "What is it, Albert?"

"I'm going jogging."

"Hold it. And don't ask, 'Hold what?' okay?" Back into the phone he said, "How do you feel this morning? About Miss Babylon?"

"Happy as a new pair of socks, by and large. But I'll admit the house seems a little too quiet."

"Come listen to the noise in this one for a couple of days, can you? God, I haven't seen you in close to a year. I'd run up there, but I've got studio stuff all day and tomorrow."

"I'll tell you what I've got," Joe said. "Computers down on my six new high-speed diesel pumps. Pump company engineer's supposed to get his German ass over here to fix them, but if the apron fills up, it's a thousand bucks an hour off my gross. Yesterday I had to fire the foreman in the truck wash, the pus-head was shaking people down for what he said were extra services. So today I got a new pus-head out there, breaking in. I got a drunk short-order cook. I got a driver waiting at the counter who already got eighty-six bucks worth of fuel in his rig and wants to charge it to a credit card that's way over limit. Know what Visa says I'm supposed to do? Yank his card and siphon his truck, but they can eat a rock. The poor fucker's got a run to finish, and a pay-off to collect . . . listen, Tomboy. If you can get loose at all, I'll have my man Freeman put his finger in the bunghole. I can catch the New Haven and be there around four-thirty."

"Only one thing I need to cancel," Tommy said. "And I'm just the boy to cancel it. How long can you stay?"

"Tonight, anyway. Here's my kraut engineer."

"*Sieg heil,*" Tommy said. "See you around four-thirty."

He'd been ignoring incoming-call signals, and as soon as he hung up, the machine started answering again. He left the speaker off, now, and said to Albert:

"Going jogging, are you?"

"With your kind permission."

"Why don't you jog on over to Ray's and see if you can transfer in?"

"For tonight? Your brother doesn't think you've gone back to hokey-pokey, does he?"

"No. But I don't think he'd enjoy you for a roomate, either."

"I'll go to Ray's then, if that's what you want."

"I hope it's what Ray wants."

"He'll split his face wide open grinning. What's going on with your brother?"

"His marriage just broke down."

"Just like yours?" Nineteen years before, Tommy had married a woman named Holly. It lasted a year.

"Nothing like mine," he told Albert.

"Did you like it?"

"It was very nice." They'd had this conversation before.

"You still like women any?"

"Albert, I love you all to pieces."

"You don't do much about it."

Albert had been underfoot for two chaste weeks, doing some cooking and housekeeping. At the end of their New Orleans days together, they had quarrelled about money, split up, lost touch. But when Albert, new in New York, made his one mournful call from jail— he'd been picked up for loitering—Tommy said to calm down, there was a bail bondsman he called in these matters who would spring Albert, who was then to get in a cab and come over. But don't come looking for action, Tommy'd said.

"You're the Dog," Albert said, agreeing.

Now Albert had a job, selling popcorn on the late shift at a gay movie house where Tommy knew the manager. And Albert had a friend. Tommy'd introduced him to Ray. It was time for Albert to move his slightly hurt feelings away.

Tommy would enjoy making his own cappuccino mornings, microwaving his own croissant, and there was Dolores to come in and clean. It was too bad about the hurt feelings, but Tommy hadn't felt like discussing with Albert the fact that he'd been celibate for all fourteen of the months that had passed since he'd sat with a young man named Bruno through the final weeks of Bruno's death from AIDS.

8

JOE AND Tommy were on their third Bloody Mary at Tommy's place when the tearass lady rang the bell, and Joe got up to watch his brother moving toward the door, thinking that Tommy'd never been able to pace himself and was looking kind of tired.

"Irene!" Tommy was the world's greatest fraud at sounding glad to see people. "And Edward Seventh. Come in neighbor lady."

Edward Seventh seemed to be the Pekinese which the tearass lady held protectively in her arms.

"You did it again, you bastard. I know you did."

"Irene, yes. Yes, I did, but only for a few minutes, and I thought you'd taken the doggy darlings out. You always do at three-thirty."

"Not today. I just got home, and the poor things were so far under the bed—and Wallace still won't come out."

"Come in. I'm so sorry. Irene, my sexy, antique brother, Joe."

"He plays that hideous thing," Irene said, coming into

the room. "And my poor pets go out of their minds."

"You're not talking about the fiddle?"

"God no, the bagpipe. They howl and cower and whine, and run under the bed and try to scratch their way through the wall." She was a rather raunchily attractive lady, with big brown eyes and jiggly skin. By the time she reached forty, in a year or two, she might be starting to get fat.

"Tommy's a great piper," Joe said. "If they heard me try, they'd crash out through the windows and fall seven stories."

"Oh God, you don't play too?"

"Have a chair and a Bloody Mary with us," Tommy said. Irene looked Joe over quite openly, pursed her lips, nodded her head, and sat down, dog in lap.

"I'll get it," Joe said, on his way to the bar to fill his own glass. The Bloody Marys were in a pitcher. "No, I don't play any more, but this coothead was a prodigy."

He fixed the drinks, and Tommy said: "Which is pretty much like being a prodigy at squeaking chalk on the blackboard, in the general view."

"Man, would I love to hear you play again," Joe said. "You keep it up?"

"Mostly on the practice chanter. I blow up the bag a couple of times a month and let the air run through to keep the pipes from drying out. But they don't play because I don't put reeds in."

"Thank the good lord." Irene drank, and held up the glass, smiling. "The Dog makes the best Bloody Mary I ever had."

"The dog?" Joe looked with curiosity at the Pekinese in Irene's lap.

"Oh, not this little pooch. I mean your brother."

"He's always been a nickname guy," Joe said. "But I never heard that one before."

The phone rang. Tommy let the machine answer, and turned up the speaker. It was someone who desperately wanted to borrow two hundred dollars to pay his rent. Tommy pushed a button, and said, into the phone: "Weep no more, Harry. You can pick it up at the Club around six." He hung up and said: "Reason I put the reeds in was to see if they'd tune okay. I'm doing a contest next month. Gathering of the clans in Nova Scotia, Joe. You want to come?"

"Hell, yes. Let's check dates when I get back to my dumb calendar."

"How about you and Edward and Wallace?" Tommy grinned at Irene. "There'll be pipe majors there from the old country. And whole bands. Massed bands. Bring the pekes, it'll make real dogs out of 'em."

"I'd give you a Bloody Mary shampoo if this didn't taste so good."

"How can you get ready for a contest?" Joe asked. "If you don't rehearse?"

"I'm only going to enter in the pibroch," Tommy said. "It's one I've been playing since I was fourteen, and I'll have a couple of days on the road, going up. I figure I can stop off in parks. Get out in the woods and run through it a few times."

"Is it the 'Lament'?" Joe asked, and Tommy nodded. "I can't tell you how much I want to hear it again."

That was when Tommy gave him a cassette he'd made the year before, saying there was some light music on it, too, tossing it to Joe and saying, "Want one, Irene?"

"Shit, man."

"Have dinner with us?"

Irene looked once again at Joe, and Tommy added, "That well-aged hunk of beef has just thrown his wife out of the house."

"I hope you opened the door first?" Irene said.

"Yep, and she landed right side up," Joe said. "Can you join us?"

"I wish I could. I've got a date."

"Serious?" Tommy inquired.

"I'm serious about wanting to sell him some bonds. He's serious about wanting to get into my pants. Hey, maybe we'll come to the X-Bar after dinner. You playing tonight?"

Tommy said sure as sweet brown sugar, and Joe said, "Let's go over to Irene's and lift up the bed, so she can get her other pup out."

When they returned to Tommy's from doing that, there were two silent young men in business suits waiting at the open front door, shoulders turned away from one another.

9

BOTH YOUNG men were named Peter, but the shorter of the two was called Pete, and they wanted to talk to Tommy in private, please.

"This is my brother," Tommy said. "Something he can't listen to?"

"Please not," said Pete, who had short-cropped, blond hair.

"If you don't mind, sir?" Said Peter, whose hair was brown, fine and razor-cut.

"Don't mind a bit." Joe picked up his new cassette. "I'm going to put on earphones and hear some piping."

"Fifteen minutes, gentlemen," Tommy said, showing them into his bedroom. "Joe and I have to eat."

"Thank you, Dog," said Pete, and the door to the bedroom closed.

Joe hooked up, deciding he'd play the light music, the dance tunes and marches, and save the "Lament" for a graver mood. Goddamn, this fat boy could make a man want to move his body. By the time the strathspey started, he'd forgot it was Tommy playing, opened his eyes, looked at his watch, and saw that twenty-five minutes had gone by. He also saw that Tommy and the two Peters were standing in the bedroom doorway. He took off the earphones, and heard the shorter one, Pete, say:

"But he got the coke free, and I paid a lot for the Irish." It had the sound of one of those arguments which, having been settled, starts over.

Tommy smiled. "It's not a matter of money, is it?"

Pete flushed.

"Is it?" Tommy asked again.

"No."

"You see, you're not fighting about money, you're fighting about manners, and Peter's apologized for his, which were atrocious. On the other hand, he had shared his stash with you that the nice man gave him, so he felt entitled to take a bottle of your single keg to the party. I can't say I blame him. It sounds too marvelous to resist."

"He might have asked me."

"But he didn't. So, now go home and make up this stupid quarrel, please." Tommy's smile this time was not to be resisted. "Okay, my friend?"

"Okay," Pete said, helpless to resist smiling back. "Would you like a bottle of the Irish?"

Tommy winked, and Peter said: "Thank you, Dog." And to Joe, "Thanks for letting us see the Dog."

Joe said he was welcome, and, as soon as the Peters had moved out: "Tommy, what's this 'Dog' shit?"

"Dog shit."

"Come on."

"It's an acronym they've tagged me with. I'm embarrassed to tell you."

"Since fucking when?"

"It's an acronym," Tommy said. "Dean of Gays."

10

OUT ON West 88th Street, Tommy thought of flagging a dear little taxi because the drivers had such a marvelous assortment of accents these days, but decided it would be funnier to ride Joe across town on the Honda. That was the way Tommy usually made his arrival at the Club, anyway, getting there in time to stow the bike and have a drink or two with the regulars at the bar before he took a break for dinner.

He walked Joe to the garage on Columbus where the

big, blue bike was parked. It was dusk. The streetlights came on, and the city seemed quiet as they went inside.

Joe smiled, seeing the motorcycle in its place beside the exit booth. "You really ride this thing to work?"

"Part of my image."

"You're not going to take it to Canada?"

Tommy stroked the seat. He loved the looks of the machine the way he loved the looks of his big espresso maker. "I've got a three-wheeled trailer for my stuff. Come on. You want to drive?"

"In New York traffic?" About what Tommy thought he'd say.

"Rather take a cab?"

"I'll ride with you." Tommy handed Joe a helmet and put on his own.

They wheeled the Honda to the street. The garage dolts didn't much care for the noise when he started it inside. Now he climbed on and pressed the starter. Joe got on behind, saying:

"Hell of a machine," and they rode off, crossed Amsterdam, got to Central Park West and turned into the Park. Tommy speeded up a little crossing the Park. There was a lovely little dip in the road, just before the east end, and he figured to give Joe a thrill when they hit it. Gunned the bike, just before the dip, and they half-way leapt it.

"Hey," Joe yelled, grabbing on tight. "Let's do it again, you prick."

"Hang on," Tommy shouted back, and braked hard for the light at Fifth Avenue.

"I think I'll walk the rest of the way," Joe said, but of course with no intention.

Traffic slowed them down going east to Second Avenue, turning and stopping in front of the X-Bar, where there were, as usual, a few people waiting to watch Tommy ride up. One of them tonight, of course, was dear Harry who needed two hundred for his rent. Tommy gave it to him in an envelope, greeted the others and said he'd see them inside.

He wheeled the Honda to the alley beside the club where the kitchen people put out garbage and kept bulky supplies. It had a locked iron gate, eight feet tall, with barbed wire across the top, and there was a shabby little goof, as always, sitting on the pavement with his back to the grating. Tommy couldn't always tell the goofs apart, but this one was Ed, for a fact. Ed got up and moved out of the way, hanging onto his bag and bottle. Ed didn't look so good.

Tommy unlocked the gate, moved the Honda into the alleyway, and locked up again. He gave Ed the obligatory dollar, and said: "Keep a bleary eye on the bike for me, Ed. Okay?"

"Not me tonight," Ed said. "I got a cold, Tommy. I'm gonna sleep at the flop."

"Who's the duty wino?"

"Hoby, but I'll wait till he gets here."

"No," Tommy said, and gave Ed another buck. "Get some cold medicine, and get in bed. I'll see Hoby. Come on, Joe, let's go in where the booze is before I grab Ed's bag."

"Who were the other parties waiting to watch your entrance?"

"My following."

"As the Dog?"

"Mostly music nuts." The people who came to the X-Bar Country and Western Club were a mix: macho young professionals from Wall Street and the ad agencies, college kids, who were caught up in the small, enduring country-music fad and wanted to feel like insiders. Some of the less flamboyant gays liked the place. "They're three-piece suiters," he told Joe. "Can't tell them from the Wall Street clucks. It's no place for a flamer. In fact," he paused at the door to say it. "There aren't any places left for the flamers. New York's gone dim."

"It's plenty bright in here," Joe said, pushing open the door. "What are we drinking?"

The answer to that was Amstel Light; beer was all Tommy allowed himself when he was working. Joe said he'd take the same, and Tommy left him with it. There was moist flesh to press and hot fives to high up and down the bar. It was part of the job, which paid a good salary and percentage, but did even the best of fellows have to do more than two beers' worth of it before supper?

He led Joe across the street to Stern's, to his table at the front window, where Terry appeared with the menu as soon as the McKay boys sat down.

"Never mind the menu," Tommy said. "I need a tartare steak."

"Sure," Terry said. "Got the first asparagus . . ."

"Cook it. Want a menu, Joe?"

Joe said raw meat and cooked asparagus sounded fine, and another beer might be worth some cool, hard thought. Then he said, reaching his big hand across the table and closing it around Tommy's wrist, "Now do we get to talk, Bub? Or are we expecting ten more people and their pooches?"

"I didn't think you minded Irene all that much."

"Didn't mind any of them. Enjoying myself, but I do want to see you."

"You want to talk about Deedee?" He watched Joe hesitate. "Why'd you marry her?"

"Man goes into his fifties with a permanent hard-on, I guess. She filled her tank at the truck stop one day. Coldest day of the year. Came inside to pay, and warm herself up with coffee, and when she went back out the car wouldn't start. She had a Porsche, still does, and it's a bad little mother on winter starts. Anyway, back indoors came Deedee, demanding to see the manager, says she must have got some rotten gas. So the suave young manager goes out, realizes the car is flooded, starts it for her with his magic foot . . ."

"And the next thing you know she's playing on his magic flute."

"Matter of fact, it wasn't that easy," Joe said. "Some guy told me she worked at the modelling school, and I bet I called six times before she'd go out with me. But . . ." He smiled. "Turned out that's how long she took to move out the guy who was living with her. I knew damn well she liked me. Know what was fun? Buying a house together and setting it up. Neither one of us had ever owned a house before."

"How bad do you feel about the way it ended?"

"I'm cooling out." Joe shook his head, sipped his beer, and seemed to have had his purge. "Tell me why the gay bars have closed."

"You can't figure it out?"

"AIDS?"

"Maybe I'm starting to know how you felt in the war."

"That could be," Joe said. "What do you do about it, Tom?"

"Live like a monk."

"For sure?"

"For damn sure." Now it was his turn to hesitate, but Joe was always the guy he could talk to, as long as they weren't fighting. "It's like an arrow sticking out between my shoulders, night and day. The friends I have. The boys I've loved. They're dying out there, Joe. And there's nothing anyone can do about it."

Joe agreed.

The food came. After Terry'd left it, Joe said: "Glad you're playing safe. Hard to do?"

"Less so than I thought. Well, hell, of course I miss it. I always was a horny customer. But, you know, it's not the fear that keeps me home."

"No?"

"It's the sadness."

It seemed to take Joe a moment to think about that. Then he half-closed his eyes and nodded, as if he knew what Tommy meant. And maybe he did.

"I'm not saying it's the blues night and day. We make a lot of loud jokes about it. I went to an AIDS funeral the other day. Black humor junction. They had an empty coffin, because the youngster's actual body'd been sent home. And the parents weren't inviting his friends to the service. So they bought this cheap coffin, and had a wake. They got skull and crossbone labels from a pharmacy supply place, and stuck them on champagne glasses. And nobody was allowed to try the coffin on for size who hadn't tested positive. It was some romp."

Joe thought about that, too. Then he said, "Yep," and

did the nod again. "How long's your casualty list? People you've known?"

"Three cities full. New York, New Orleans, San Francisco. Guys I've been close to? Seven so far. Some of them going way back. Every month or two you hear another name. Frank tested positive, Gary's gone to bed and won't get up again."

"Yep."

"Fletch died in Ireland."

"Tell me about Fletch."

"A smile I'll never forget. A quiet, radiant man. Studious. Serene. I can show you that smile in a photograph Fletch sent, speaking of living like a monk. Fletch went all the way. Franciscan. Robed and tonsured. And he was fine when I rode him out to Idlewyld on the bike. No luggage to speak of, because he'd given away all his worldly goods. Happy. A hand on my waist lightly. Singing in Latin. So it seemed like he'd made his peace, and his bargain, too, didn't it? Six months later . . . you can carry that goddamn crazy virus around in you for two or three years before it starts to get active and you start feeling sick."

He shouldn't have said it. Stoopid. No question what Big Broth was hesitating about this time, and no way of stopping the damn question.

"You had yourself tested, Tommy?"

"No, goddamn it, have you?"

"Me?"

"You've been sleeping with Deedee. She's been partying with Victor. How do you know who else big Vic parties with?"

Joe seemed about to say something, changed his mind and kept it simple.

"Life in the minefields."

"So what's your preference? You want to know for sure you're strapped onto a self-propelled stretcher, moving slowly onto a mine? I'll take as much ignorance as I can get, for as long as I can have it."

"But you're feeling all right?"

"Hell, yes. Look at me."

Joe was turning out to be Mr. Hesitation himself. Decisive fella. The decisive fella was looking him in the eye, but he didn't hold it long. There was a nice yellow egg yolk like an eyeball in the middle of Joe's plate of raw beef. It was probably a fierce, strong-minded egg yolk, but it didn't have a chance. Decisive Joe stared it down. Then he asked, "Nobody recovers?"

"I've heard some rumors of remissions, but I think it's drumming on the tombstone. I don't know of any. I'm going to say nobody recovers."

"God."

"Exactly. Dear old God's final solution to the sodomy problem. He's been working on it for centuries."

"You figure Lot was gay?"

"Nobody ever said his wife was female."

Joe smiled at that, took a good big swallow of beer, and mashed up his yellow egg-eye, ready to eat.

This was a damned handsome old fart of a brother Tommy McKay had, with the straight, thick black hair and bronze skin. Renegade Great Grandad McKay, who'd lammed out of Scotland after what must have been a murder, had married an Indian, who must have been some kind of renegade herself. And there she was, looking out of Joe's black eyes.

Tommy grinned to make the hard, high-boned face light up with its own rough, wicked smile, and what a pair of damn shoulders.

The renegades had several children, exact number unrecorded, before Great Grandad got himself knocked off fighting for the Confederacy. One of these children was a farmer, harness maker and auctioneer of cattle and horses, who went to Scotland to find a wife and brought her back to Glasgow, Kentucky. That's where Joe's and Tommy's father was born. Dad grew up to inherit the auction barn, lose it in the Depression and go back to the family farm, now almost inside the city limits. There he was established as a mild eccentric, sought out as a bagpiper and drinking buddy, and envied for the warmth and hospitality of his wife, 'a remarkably beautiful lady whose parents had come to Glasgow, Kentucky, from Sweden. Tommy'd adored her. And Tommy'd got her looks.

As a boy, Tommy'd been all golden and cheery-looking, which people liked, but now he was fat and cheery-looking and dyed the gold into his hair, and people liked his looks in a different way. They thought he was jovial, dumbasses. All his life he'd wished he looked like his fucking brother, formidable enough so that Joe seldom had to be anything but affable. With all that, there was some mysterious point of resemblance which made people unsurprised to learn that Tommy and Joe were brothers, stupid eyebrows or something, and when Tommy talked straight his voice and accent were just like Joe's, who was now ready to give up on the AIDS-test inquisition, and wanted to know what Tommy heard from Holly.

Holly was this nutty broad to whom Tommy had been

married for one absolutely preposterous year, and by
whom he'd had a fireball son called Little Joe, now sixteen, six-foot-two, and kind of an enigma. Sometimes he
was open and affectionate. Sometimes he was a wary,
withdrawn little coot. Maybe it figured.

"Holly married number four about a year ago. Jesus,
we have been out of touch, you and I."

"Way Deedee wanted it. Fought about it often enough,
too. Where's Ms. Holly living now?

"Hawaii. Right next door to Sweet Leilani, probably.
The new guy's a professional surfer. Gives lessons."
Tommy'd never seen the man, but he had an image of
sunlight on muscles. Holly was queer for muscles, of
which Tommy'd even had a few himself back in those
years, though never like Joe's. And that brought to mind
a question Tommy'd always wanted to ask, and never
had the balls. He didn't ask it.

"Little Joe will be going back and forth from school to
Hawaii? That's some damn trip."

Little Joe was a basketball hotshot at a New England
prep school that favored jocks. Come to remember, it
was Uncle Joe who started the kiddo playing the game.
"Short vacations, he comes down here. Been twice now.
I had to clean up my lifestyle quite a bit the first time.
Didn't have much style left to clean the second."

"Come on," Joe said. "He knows about you."

"Doesn't mean he likes to see it. I think he kind of
sensed that things had changed when he came down last.
He was less edgy with me. We had a pretty good time."

"Going to stop off and see him when you go to Canada?"

"Planning on it, but I haven't checked with him."

"I wonder if they'd let me take him fishing? I haven't seen Joe this year."

"They're strict. And he'll be running track, but ask."

"Maybe I could catch a meet. I'd love to see him run." Joe had always loved Little Joe like his own. Matter of fact, the lad looked more and more like his uncle as he got older. Tommy swallowed hard, and asked the question after all. It had been a burr up his ass for seventeen years.

"Joe, did you ever fuck Holly?"

"Shit." Tommy knew he wouldn't lie. "Yeah, Thomas. After you broke up, I hope I don't need to add."

"Little Joe's starting to look like you."

"Huh-uh. Nossir. Holly was two months pregnant when we got together."

"We didn't know she was pregnant at all when we split."

"Little Joe's your kid all the way, Tommy, and I envy you. I surely do. Now listen . . ."

"I'm going to hear all about the great romance?"

"Let's clear it up. I was working at the motor pool at Fort Eustace . . ."

"And making big dough, renting out jeeps and staff cars on the side."

"My days as a crook," Joe said. "Major Tosca already had the business going. Old man had a sign on his desk saying, 'We're Number Three'. And Bill Harper, guy I replaced, briefed me right away. I tell you, Harper hated to leave as much I hated being there. I was line company, and wanted to retire that way, but shit, my outfit was deactivated, so they filled my hand with grease. It was get into John Tosca's operation, or blow the whistle on him . . ."

"How much did you make? Enough to retire and buy into a truck stop, apparently."

"I'm not proud of it," Joe said. "Anyway, one day when I got home from the grease pits—you remember my apartment, off the post? —Holly was waiting in the living room. She still had the key from when you guys visited. I asked her why she didn't call first, and it was because she didn't want to talk about being pregnant on the phone. That's what she'd come to tell me, and ask what to do about you. You didn't know yet you were going to be a pop."

Tommy didn't say anything.

"I told her you'd be glad. She thought so, too, but she was afraid you'd pressure her about getting back together. She wanted to have the baby, but . . ."

"Okay, okay." Tommy wanted him to speed it up.

"You want to hear this?"

He did and he didn't . . . "Let's clear it up," he said.

"She stayed a week. Nothing happened the first night, except we drank a bunch. The next morning I was in the kitchen in my pajama bottoms, barefoot, making coffee. Holly came in in her nightgown, hungover."

What kind of cherry-bellied masochist was Tom McKay? This kind: "I can do the rest myself," he said. "Small, dirty blonde with dirty eyes, and those lovely teats pretty near falling out. The nighties were always loose up top. That beautiful little flat ass. She said, 'Gawd, I'm one hungover girl,' and slipped her bare foot over yours, and there was just enough vulnerability in the way she did it to make you grab everything she had, top and bottom. She turned around and sagged back into you, and you played with her stuff a minute and goosed her into the bedroom."

"No," Joe said slowly. "We hit the kitchen floor. Neither one of us could wait." He paused and said, "Like I told you, she stayed a week, Tommy. I hope you're not offended."

That was a stiff word for Joe to use, stiffer than, never mind what it was stiffer than. "I hope I'm not," Tommy said, and what should a maraschino-belly do now? How about a nice smile?

"I even thought of trying to marry Holly myself that week. So I could help raise the baby."

"Joe, the childless macho man."

"Tommy the family man, Dean of Gays."

11

TOMMY HAD gone to change into his working clothes. Joe knew the drill: jeans, suede Wellingtons and a cowboy shirt.

He sat at a table beside the empty bandstand, thinking about the time seventeen years before when he'd been a crook and cheating with a woman who was still, technically, his brother's wife. Holly. She was one of a trio of singers who called themselves The Pepper Sisters, though, of course, they weren't related. Holly was the screwball one, the clown. God, she had a cute body. Tommy'd worked shows with the trio in New Orleans and one night, Tommy said, Holly'd dared him to come to her bed and prove he was able. Wasn't the first time Tommy'd made it with a female, but it sure was different. He and Holly'd been crazy about one another. At first. But the guests at the wedding had a pool as to how many weeks the marriage would last, and the kid who drew 57 won it . . . Joe reckoned that if he were that age again, and dealt the same cards, he'd play them the same way. So if he wasn't proud of it, he wasn't feeling much guilt, either, was he? The answer was probably not in the bottom of the glass of bourbon he was staring into.

"Lose something in there?"

It was Irene, the jiggly, tearass lady with her richly suited date, a silver-haired, prime-of-life party, clearly prospering, who knew who his manicurist was, not just his barber. Not too displeased with himself, Arnold Oberlin.

12

WELL, LOOKEE there, if it wasn't three merrymaking merrymakers, clapping when Tommy led the dunderheads onto the stand in their musicmaking musicmaker country drag. Tommy waved a friendly fiddle at Irene, whose date had the sleek face and forehead of a large trout, while the dunders sat down and set up like good little boys, plugged in, and let Tommy tune them up. Then he went to the mike, noted that the joint was packed, whooped once, yodelled twice and hollered, "Hidee, nei-ghbors. Let's party."

Some of the customers hollered back, "Hi, Tommy," and at a couple of tables were dear boys whom he knew who hollered, "Hi, Dog, let's party," and did some barking and howling.

"I'm gonna warm up the redneck Stradivarius with a little bluegrass for my brother Joe—'The Old Hen Cackled and the Rooster's Gonna Crow'—now who's gonna get up and show him how to dance?"

The redneck Stradivarius did indeed have a stripe of red-lacquered ebony set into the back of the fingerboard, though it wasn't modelled from a Strad. It was a Maggini type that Tommy'd had made, strung with steel and just plain loud, though a man could play it pretty when he wanted.

They knocked off "Old Hen" smartly, though Jeff was having intonation problems with the mandolin. Tommy let him know about it in a curt whisper before he turned, stomped, waved off the applause and did his next crowd-pleaser, which was to tell them the story of the great 1878 horse race down in Kentucky, between Molly and Tenbrooks, crediting Bill Monroe, before he played and sang it for them: "Women all laughing/ Children all crying/ Men all hollering/ and Tenbrooks flying . . ."

Applause, laughter and time for a change of mood:

"Our new album's gonna be dedicated to the man people call the best bluegrass fiddler ever lived, Scotty Stoneman, I heard him play a cuple of times, and he was just awesome, and I do a lot of Scotty's songs as close to the way he did them as I can get.

"But I have to tell you that Scotty was just about as awesome with a bottle as he was with a fiddle, and died real young. Died the day he couldn't find anything else to drink, and tried aftershave. It's a hell of a way to die, neighbors. So now we're gonna play one of Scotty Stoneman's great ones, 'Lee Highway Blues.' I want you to remember it. And lay off the Aqua Velva, promise me now."

Then, when they'd done "Lee Highway" and done it right, done it in the way Tommy was going to want it in the album, he called "Foggy Mountain Breakdown," and they fired off a hell of a bunch of choruses to end the first set.

He sat down with Joe and the others, and was introduced to troutface.

"You play very skillfully," said The Face, who looked like he went to a jewelry store to have his silver hair done.

You choose your words very carefully, Tommy thought, but he said: "I'm a skillful fella."

"May I see your instrument?"

The one I play on or the one I play with? was the answer, of course, but Tommy shrugged it away and handed Arnold Oberlin the fiddle. Arnold examined it and handed it back: "You had it made?"

"Couple of years ago."

"I have three violins. The newest was made in 1780. The oldest, well, it's a Guarnerius."

"A Joseph?" Maybe Tommy had this gentleman wrong. "You play?"

"No. I collect."

Oh, Christ. "Your collection ever get itself played on?"

"Not the Joseph, but the other two are out on loan. To serious musicians."

"Ah, serious," Tommy said. "Gee, if there's anything I admire, it's a serious musician. Don't you feel that way, Joe?"

"I can't stand those fucking comical musicians," Joe said agreeably.

Irene moved in fast. "Are you going to play 'Sally Goodin' for me tonight, Tommy?"

"You know I'm not, pretty lady."

"Please? Just this once?"

Tommy smiled and shook his head.

"But why not?" Asked Arnold Oberlin.

Tommy hesitated, and then decided to give the fine gentleman a straight answer. " 'Sally Goodin' is a Texas fiddling specialty, and Irene's from Texas. I know the song, but I don't know all the variations. She'd be disappointed in the way I played it."

Arnold Troutsnout got out a beautiful big, black billfold, pinseal, wow, gold corners, lookathat, and said: "I'll give you twenty bucks to play it anyway."

"I'll give you forty to quit asking me," Tommy told him and damned if Irene didn't punch him once, hard, out of sight, just below the rib cage. "All right, darling," Tommy said. "Why don't you try some other requests so we can keep on playing this nice game?"

"I got one," Joe said. "You still play 'How Mountain Girls Can Love'?"

"Haven't played it for years, and I doubt the other guys would know it." He smiled at his brother, cautious of Joe asking for that one. The song belonged to Carrie. Joe's long-ago first wife. Used to tease her with it. Tenderly. Tommy hadn't played it since Carrie died in the fire, and if Joe really wanted to hear it, the bourbon must be getting into his tear ducts. Tommy, who'd seen beaucoup of weak men crying didn't want to add a strong one to his list. Didn't really want to fuss with Irene, either, or Fish the Face. So he jumped up, ruffled Joe's hair, flung himself onto the bandstand and grabbed the mike.

"Sit still, peons," he said, meaning the other band members. "Break's not over yet. Finish your foul liquids. I'm gonna tell these people all about my brother Joe, sitting right there, now there is one slick businessman, that big hunk, lushing it up, wondering what would happen if he put his hand on Irene's knee.

"Now, it's a nationally known fact that thirty-four percent of all truck drivers are gay, you all know that, don't you? So what's my big, smart brother do? He may not be gay, but he's slick enough to open up The Trucker's Tea Room, the dearest little truck stop in the whole, wide, wicked world. It's right up there in Connecticut, beside a babbling brook, and you should hear what that naughty brook babbles about, and every diesel pump has a flower bed around it.

"And Joe bustling around in his Mother Hubbard and gay deceiver to greet the boys and show them inside, where they talk about color-coordinating your seat covers and truck window curtains, and how to get comfortable driving in a sarong. I mean only at The Trucker's Tearoom do they have bidets in the men's room.

"And there's a gypsy boy to read the tea leaves, X-rated tea leaves, of course, but not all the drivers who go there

are gay, I mean there's nifty little deviations, too, like the
ones who are just plain mad for their big, strong trucks?

"So there's private pumps curtained off for ones like
that, who like to grab the nozzle and unscrew the little
pink gastank cap, and . . . ooooh . . ."

He was going good. He had them laughing pretty well,
and Joe about doubled up; sometimes when they were
younger he'd make Joe laugh till it really hurt, and
Tommy wouldn't mind giving him a dose of that right
now, either, but anyway, it felt good, doing this kind of
number now and then, making it up as he went along.
He told them about Pierre Bon Chance, the gourmet
short-order cook, inventor of the goatsmilk cheese-
burger *au poivre,* who could also make chili so bland the
lesbian drivers used it for face cream, and speaking of
the lezzies, with their special place at the counter where
the sign said "For Professional Ladies Only," Joe was
planning to keep them segregated that way ever since
the big fight broke out between them and the interior
decorating freaks over what color Joe's new carpet
ought to be. He acted out the fight, with the gay male
drivers swinging their purses, the gay females pulling
hair and punching. "Whew, that was just the other day,
and I mean they really wrecked the joint, it's closed now
for repairs, otherwise we could all drive up tomorrow
for a sightseeing tour, come on peons. 'Nough words,
let's make some music."

Got a nice hand.

Exhausted? God, no. So exhilarated he started off the
next set with "The Devil's Dream," and played it so fast
Jeff couldn't keep up on the mandolin, had to set it down
and keep time clapping.

By the time that set was done, Tommy was all glowing and sweaty, and had to go back and sluice off in the private john you entered from the office, dry off and put on a fresh shirt. He'd probably do it again before the night was over. And he'd probably decide it was time to audition some mandolin players.

13

JUST AFTER three o'clock in Tommy's apartment, where he was trying to cool out with a Beefeaters and tonic, and Joe already had his shirt off, came a knock at the door. Tommy's intuition said *Irene.*

Tommy's intuition knew what it was talking about.

"Cuddle me," she said. "Comfort me."

"Just like you did me at the club?" Tommy shook a fist, but he was laughing. "Defending your date."

"Defending my sale." Irene reached into her purse and got out a sheet of paper from a legal pad, which she waved at them. "It's Arnold's shopping list. Congratulate me, gentlemen."

"Outstanding," yelled Joe, pretty drunk by now.

"And did the little girl make the great big sale by using the method referred to earlier?" Tommy asked.

Irene raised her eyebrows and did a fast pout.

"Time *honored,*" hollered drunken Joe.

But when Tommy tried to get them sitting together, so

that he could slip off and leave them to whatever they might like to be left to, Joe wouldn't stop capering until he'd got Irene capered out the door.

"She asked for a cuddle," Tommy said. "I thought you might want to oblige."

"Yes, brother Tom," Joe said. "But that is what the limeys call a buttered bun. I've had a great time, baby, but all I want to cuddle now is a bourbon and pillow."

14

THERE WAS a hell of an air raid going on in Naples, and one of the bombs went off so close to where Joe lay dreaming that it shook the building. Then it yanked Joe's wrist, nearly pulled him off the bed in Tommy's study, and yelled:

"Get up, you bastard. I hate it about you fucking Holly."

"Jesus," Joe said. There was a digital clock across the room that read 5:55, and Tommy had the wild look of a man who hasn't been to bed for agonizing.

"Get up." Tommy pulled him to his feet, turned loose the wrist, hit Joe in the chops and knocked him back onto the bed.

"Tommy."

"I'll Tommy you, all cock and no balls. Get up." Tommy took a slap at him, which Joe ducked.

"You're making me mad, Tommy."

"Why wasn't Holly a buttered bun? Answer me, prick."

With a yell, Joe set his hands and feet, pushed off hard, head low, to butt Tommy in the stomach. Tommy went back, and Joe reached after him and caught the lapels of his brother's dressing gown.

"You don't want to fight me, lardass," he said, let go of the lapels, and clipped the fat man a couple under the ear with the edge of his hand. Punched him in the gut. "Do you?"

"I don't care. I hate you." Tommy seemed close to tears.

"Well, you're a pretty drastic piece of ape shit, aren't you? Christ, you sound like a six-year-old. Let me get my clothes and get out of here."

"The sooner the better, pig's cunt," said Tommy, recovering himself.

15

THE McKAY boys didn't communicate a hell of a lot after Joe's New York visit. Joe felt bad about it, because he realized, riding back on the train, that Tommy'd gone temporarily bonkers during the night, sitting up, brooding, drinking. Tommy'd been overcharged from the evening performance, from teasing with Irene, from the family talk earlier. Tommy hadn't known how to turn himself off. Joe'd seen him that way before, close to hysterical, childish, brilliant, to hell with it.

Nevertheless, Joe arm-wrestled himself into leaving a message on Tommy's machine next day, *"Hey, bub, let's forget it. Give me a call."* Wondered if Tommy heard that one over his loudspeaker, maybe made a joke to whoever was listening with him, and declined to answer.

Joe planned his fishing trip, sent in money to hold a campsite for the third weekend in May. Landlocked salmon were exactly the same fish as Atlantic salmon, but since the landlocks didn't come in from the sea fasting, to spawn, they fed all year round. Still, late May was when the water temperature and other stats were right.

16

"OBERLIN'S LENDING me his Jag," Irene said. "Come on. Let's take the dogs out in the country."

It was Sunday. Two of the peons, one of them the new mandolin, were down with flu. Tommy'd already cancelled rehearsal. Loose-ends McKay said, "Of course, darling. I'll just slip into my tweeds and take the sword cane, in case of brigands."

"How about the tire iron?"

"Why, hell, that'd do her just about right now."

But it wasn't until they were halfway to New Haven that he tumbled to what the sly and slimy bitch was doing to him. They were easing along, with Elvis singing "Heartbreak Hotel" on the tape player, when the cartoon light bulb in his head came on.

He let the song end, turned down the volume, and said in his smoothest, most caressing voice, "You are a totally horrid cunt."

"What?"

Good. He'd startled her. "You're taking me to see Joe, aren't you?"

"Well, Tommy. I've been wanting to see that truck stop."

"It's Sunday, but you know he's on shift because you called him up."

"I didn't say you were coming, too."

"We better go back for that tire iron."

"Nonsense, and you'd both better behave or I'll sic the doggies on you."

Tommy turned his head to look at Edward Seventh and Wallace Warfield, two little balls of fur on the back seat, wriggling with pleasure over being noticed, and said, "I can see I have no choice."

17

FREEM, JOE's deputy manager, stuck his curly, Syrian-Brazilian head into the office, and said: "There's a lady and a fat guy in a Jag, waiting to see you. By the west door."

"I'll be damned. I know who the lady and the fat guy are, but where in hell did they steal a Jag?"

Tommy was out of the car when Joe got there, and a couple of shouts of *asshole of the month,* and *scrambled shit for brains,* and a big bear hug were what were called for.

"Please, gentlemen," Irene said. "Your language." And the dogs yipped, because there was excitement going on, so Irene told them to watch their language, too.

18

LOVELY. TOMMY'D been shuddering at Irene's anticipation of truck stop ham and eggs with hashbrowns, but the good Joe had brought them instead to a tablecloth joint called Tremaine's for swordfish baked in milk, served on pureed sorrel and a large, heart-shaped *crouton.*

Chef Paul, whom Tommy would have dearly loved to tickle under his third chin, grateful to anyone that much fatter than himself, was, in fact, standing at their table, explaining to Joe how the sorrel was done.

"I got the swordfish fine," Joe'd said. "But my sorrel wasn't tart enough," and Chef Paul said to try dry vermouth instead of the white wine.

"Who've you been cooking for?" Dear Irene wanted to know, when the Chef had left. Irene's motives in bringing them up here were mixed like salted nuts. Tommy could tell she'd wanted to see Joe again on her own behalf.

"Well, there was a lady named Marie," Joe said, "until last weekend, when she went back to Colorado to teach spring quarter."

"Somebody told Joe that women who loved to eat were sensual in other departments, too," Tommy said. "Joe was standing at the door, waiting for cooking school to open next morning."

"Bullshit," Joe said. "I'm a natural born gourmet cook, though I admit I do like to see a lady enjoy her food."

"What else do you like to see her do?" Asked Irene, the incautious.

"Well," Joe said, deadpan, "I kind of like to watch her take off all her clothes, lie down on her back, and put both feet behind her head."

Tommy whooped, and how long since Ms. Shameless had actually blushed?

The rest of the time they talked about Tommy's trip to Canada for the Gathering of the Clans, and the bagpipe competition. He'd be leaving New York Wednesday after next, stop off at Little Joe's school, and arrive at the Gathering Saturday to play Sunday.

Joe said he felt stupid and cross at himself. If he'd kept in touch, he could have fixed up his own vacation schedule to be in Nova Scotia the same weekend, and then driven back down to Maine for the fishing. But as it was, Freem had the next two weeks off to visit family in Rio, and the truck stop wouldn't run if both Joe and Freem were away.

"By the time I'm able to start North, you'll be all done playing," he said.

"Mmmm. Well," Tommy said, thinking. "Want to write me down the directions to your fishing camp?"

"Could you come there?"

"On the way back. If I don't have to sleep on the ground."

19

TOM MCKAY worked his big, fat, musical buns into the usual lather Tuesday night, and put them to bed at 3:00 A.M.. When he got up Wednesday, he had three things to do before leaving the city.

One was to see Jamie Ponchatoula's little friend Brandon, who'd got his collarbone busted night-before-last wrestling with a Norwegian sailor. Tommy took him a couple of books and a bottle of Spanish brandy, and stayed long enough at the furnished room to cheer the sucker up.

After that, Tommy and the peons had a photo date for an album-cover picture, with a photographer Tommy'd agreed to try out, a new dear boy in town. He decided to cancel the third thing, which was lunch with London Bob, the Gay Deejay, for whom Tommy just wasn't in a jolly mood. He went to the bank, stopped to buy some clarinet reeds, and was clear to leave for New Hampshire, where he'd booked a room at the pretty Fritchie Inn, a quarter-mile from Little Joe's prep school.

The clarinet reeds were for use tomorrow morning,

when he was slated to talk about Southern music and play some of it at a school assembly.

As a younger man, Tommy'd made his living for a time playing Dixieland clarinet in New Orleans, before he learned there was a better living to be made playing the fiddle music he grew up with and felt more deeply. And he liked swing very well, too, and had played some of that professionally on piano in his New Orleans days. For the preppies, he'd play some on all three instruments, and try to show how the three kinds of music weren't all that unrelated—take a song like "The Bucket's Got a Hole in It," and do it bluegrass, Dixie and swing. It was a kind of show he'd put on at Fritchie each year Little Joe was there.

Riding the Honda through Connecticut on a soft, sweet Spring afternoon, he found himself thinking pleasurably about the school's big Steinway in the auditorium, thinking maybe he'd buy himself a piano this year and write some songs. He was one hell of a self-taught sight reader and improviser, and sometimes wondered whether, if he'd had the training, he might not have made a concert pianist. Well, scag my bag, Mr. Motorcycle McKay, and is it the piano that you deeply love? No sir. Not like the pipe.

There was nothing like the Great Highland Bagpipe.

You tickled, touched and ravished a piano with both hands. You wooed a clarinet with lips and tongue and fingers. Embraced, stroked, practically thrust into a fiddle. But you played a bagpipe standing at attention.

You played it outdoors, because there was no way to mute or soften it. You played continuously, because the stream of air going into the chanter never stopped. It was not like playing any other wind instrument, because your breath was separated from the notes being sounded. Your breath went through the blowpipe, keeping the bag full. Your left arm squeezed out the air. And the three drones played untouched, while your hands reached out to the holes in the chanter, where the notes were, almost an arm's length away. The other instruments yielded to a man. The bagpipe held him away. It dignified him.

Dignified his dong, Dog, now will you veer me this crawlin' Caddy, and cut the sandy salamander close, give him a thrill, shit, you call that close? Who cares? It was dandy to be riding free of the shriek and stink of the city, on his way to a lovely, quiet town to see his big young lion of a son.

The headmaster would have let Joe come out for dinner, but Tommy preferred taking the kid out to lunch after the program, when Joe might be feeling his dad was okay.

Tired from the ride when he reached the Inn, Tommy ate lightly, had a couple of cognacs with the innkeeper in front of the wood fire in the library, agreed to write the hairy hamster an endorsement to use in his ads, went to bed early, and woke up feeling fresher than he had in a long time.

He dressed with care, wearing a light flannel shirt in the McKay tartan, his new camelhair jacket, gray flannels and desert boots. The clothes were a pleasure to wear.

He went down to the dining room with a dumb smile on his face and felt it turn into a dumb grin when he saw who was waiting to have breakfast with him.

"Hey, Dad." Little Joe jumped up, ran across the room, and gave Tommy a hug. There'd been a time when the kid didn't do things like that.

"Hey, hey, kiddo." Tommy hugged him back, pushing his son away so he could have a look, and said: "You look more like your idiot uncle every day."

"How is my idiot uncle? He called the Head. He wanted to take me fishing, but it's during the week."

"He's going to take me fishing instead," Tommy said. "I wish we could have done it together. Listen, coming down off the river, maybe Joe and I can stop here together."

Little Joe said that would be absolutely great.

They sat down, and ordered fresh-squeezed ojay, bacon and eggs and popovers, coffee, and Tommy could just barely believe it, though he wasn't going to question it. Little Joe was an affectionate enough kid, but there'd been a time when he seemed gloomy about it, a little smart-ass, too, a boy with reservations about his father for obvious enough reasons. Today Little Joe was sunny and puppy-like, as if he'd resolved his doubts. Tommy could only be grateful.

They rode over to school side-by-side, Joe on his ten-speed, Tommy with the Honda in low gear. A group of Joe's friends were waiting for them outside the auditorium, a beautiful, well-groomed bunch in their coats and ties, several of whom Tommy'd met in the years before. Were they, would you say, glad to see Joe's Dad? Yowsuh.

Mr. McKay! Welcome back. They were all over him and his motorcycle, one of them seizing his cased violin when Tommy got it out of the trailer, another the clarinet. They were more or less pushing him up the stairs, at the top of which he had to stop to shake hands with the tall headmaster and the giggly guy who taught music. Giggly was new this year, and what a nice job it must be.

It couldn't go any way but well. Giggly made a rather fruity introduction, based on his having borrowed a couple of Tommy's albums from Little Joe the night before, and Tommy responded with a grandiose run and a big announcement chord on the Steinway.

"That's me, oh Lord," he sang out. "Standing in the need of prayer." Trotted to the front of the stage and clapped his hands.

"Preppies, jocks and yuppies," he began, and paused to let the boys applaud themselves. "What you're looking at is a genuine, down-home, New York hillbilly ..." And he was off, talking about Appalachian music, singing some lyrics, demonstrating melodies and variations on the fiddle, dancing a few steps, talking evolution. Picked the fiddle like a mandolin to accompany himself singing country blues, dived onto the piano bench and pumped those keys, getting them to do the bucket with him:

"Bucket's got a hole in it," he'd shout, and then play an 8-bar break and stop, so they could shout back:

"I hear you knockin' but you can't come in."

He showed them how that was country on the fiddle, and then picked up the clarinet for the first time to play it Dixie.

He'd been putting out energy the way he always did when he performed, had long since put aside the camel-hair jacket, had the flannel shirt soaked through. Whew. He sat on the piano bench, back to the keyboard, facing all those bright eyes, playing the clarinet, and they still heard him knocking but he couldn't come in. Then he swung the same song on the piano, and was ready to get on to the next thing, which was more Dixie.

"The song's called 'High Society', " he said, and played the melody on clarinet. Whew. He decided on a piano reprise, and showed them what was going to come next, playing melody with his left hand, and playing in the treble the traditional obligato. Then he stood up with the clarinet.

"Here's the same obligato on the instrument it was originally played on, by Alfonse Picou. Maybe the first famous sustained solo in jazz history." He started playing the great, nonstop line of music and, toward the end, caught himself cheating, cutting it into phrases, about to run out of breath. Puzzling.

Managed to finish it strong, hoping he didn't show the fear that had begun to chill him. His legs felt wavery, and his feet were ice cold. His stomach was heaving, not violently but deeply. He sat down, letting the applause buy him recovery time, but he wasn't really recovering, only holding on.

He'd promised Little Joe he'd finish the lecture with his rouser, "Devil's Dream," on the fiddle, damn it, and he sat still for a minute, pumping himself up to do it. Okay. At least you didn't need lungs to play the fiddle.

He got through it because he had so many times before, though never like this, never trembling. There was a real ovation, Lord love you boys. The Head shook his hand, and invited him to lunch, which Tommy, sitting once again on the piano bench, declined. He disjointed the clarinet and cased it. He cased the violin, and

Little Joe, who'd come up on stage, took the instruments to carry.

"Dad, you were great. Better even than last year."

Hollow Tommy found a smile, and they walked out together into sunlight that seemed to have lost its warmth.

"Dad, you know what I'd like?"

"You name it, Joe boy."

"Could I spend the summer with you in New York?"

"You want to, Joe? We can, we can see what your mother says. Sure."

"Well, I mean the first part of the summer. Then going to this basketball camp in Colorado in August. I could go to Hawaii from there, if you think I should."

"I'd love to have you with me, all or any part of it," Tommy said, hoping the infinity of sadness that he felt didn't show on his face or sound in his voice. Shortness of breath, dear Jesus, was often the first symptom of the onset. He didn't want to think the word AIDS with Joe there, and kept pushing it away.

"Dad, you must be tired after putting on a show like that," Little Joe said.

20

"COME ON, Dog. You can run short of breath for a lot of reasons other than PCP," Bill Meacham said.

Tommy had phoned from New Hampshire, and then ridden back down here to Cambridge to see Bill, whom he'd known for years. The papers sometimes wrote of Bill as "the AIDS doctor"; he'd cancelled a two o'clock lecture to medical students to get Tommy into his schedule. "It could be a simple cold coming on. Or bronchitis. You ever smoke?"

"No, not really."

"You haven't any other symptoms except feeling tired, which is natural for a man who works at the pace you do. Been getting any older lately?"

Tommy smiled, but he said: "My gut tells me, 'Babe, you've got it. Start living with it.'"

"I'll put your blood test on rush. Don't start living with anything till we find out Monday."

"I'll call in and ask, okay?"

"Okay, but if it's positive, I'll want to keep you here for some more lab work. Want to spend the weekend with me? I've got a guest room."

"Thanks, Bill, no. I want to go riding."

"North? On a motorcycle? It's a bad idea, Tommy."

"I'd go nuts, sitting still and waiting. But would you prescribe some feel-goods for me? Dexamils and Quaaludes?"

Bill hesitated, nodded and said, "You got 'em, Tom."

Tommy noticed Bill wasn't calling him Dog any longer.

21

Tommy made it to Bar Harbor, Maine, Thursday night, in a state of numbness produced by motion, fear and fatigue. He took a Quaalude, and drank himself quickly to sleep at the motel.

In the morning he went on, still numb, to the Canadian National Park on the Bay of Fundy, which has the highest tides in the world. He'd called ahead for a room at the Park's Hotel, and the second morning got up early and rode to Moncton, to watch the tide roar in over red mud, cresting six feet high as it came.

He sat on his bike, watching. It was still a quarter-mile from shore, and he could see, out there on the flat, a man on a motorcycle, with that crushing first wave coming towards him, trying to ride away from it. A fat man. The wheel was spinning, digging into the mud, deeper and deeper, until the bike disappeared and the man turned toward the incoming rush of tide, walked toward it, and he disappeared, too.

That was a nice, straightforward, jerk-level piece of Dexamil hallucinating, compared to what started, intermittently, when he got to Pictou, where the Gathering of the Clans had its headquarters. Pictou was full of kilts. Tommy's kilt was in the trailer, along with the bagpipe he wasn't going to play. He decided not to unpack the stuff at all, but his father's voice said quite sternly that Tommy must wear the kilt, so Tommy went into the men's room at a filling station and changed.

He was seventeen, a secretly troubled boy with a smile that fooled 'em all, but he went back and forth from that to his real age of fifty-five, and to knowing what the secret was this time. So he took another Dexamil to get rid of the feeling that he was already dear old dead.

He parked the bike.

People were moving in the direction indicated by an arrow that had "Pictou Park" painted on it. Tommy moved with them, reached the park, and stopped to watch some muscular jocks tossing the caber.

The caber looked like a sawed-off telephone pole. It was eighteen feet long, weighed over a hundred pounds, and was tossed with both hands, starting with them down between the knees, and the tosser in a crouch. As he straightened up, he heaved the pole up and forward, so that the caber made a half turn, touched ground upright, and landed with what had been the bottom end pointing away from the contestant. Distance wasn't the point. The straightest throw won. A perfect one was called "twelve o'clock."

Tommy'd fooled around with it, but it was Joe who had the strength and the knack. Tommy waited and watched. It would be Joe's turn next. He could see Joe at the head of the line. He could remember that he and Joe had gone to some Highland Games in Florida thirty-five years ago, where Joe won everything—the caber, the weight toss, weight throw, sheaf throw and hammer— while Tommy swept the solo piping events. They'd come away with six hundred bucks in prize money, Tommy in his kilt, Joe in uniform.

"Tom. Tommy McKay." It was Uncle Henry, Dad's favorite brother.

"Over here, McKay," said the same voice. It was Ben Forbes, a retired pipe major with whom Tommy's studied the several times he'd been to Scotland. Old grizzled Ben, with his twinkling eyes, who dearly loved a party.

"Major Forbes." He'd almost called him Uncle Henry. He'd better watch himself. But this crowd was full of the friends and relatives of his youth, dressed up Scotch for the annual games in Glasgow, Kentucky, wasn't it? He was pretty addled, but sort of happy with it. "You're competing today?"

Clearly the Major was, for he had on the complete ceremonial costume—tunic, vest, kilt, sporan, plaid and bonnet with a sprig of heather, in the yellow-green, dark green, black and yellow of his clan.

"I've a daughter in the dancing just now. Will we see her?"

Cousin Alice McKay was dancing? This weirdly comforting thing came and went. In a minute he'd see Mom.

Sure. Tommy asked Major Forbes again if he'd be competing.

"I am that, and saw your own name on the list for the Pibroch open class tomorrow. What will you play?"

"Afraid I'm going to scratch myself," Tommy said. "I'm not up to it this year."

"Keeping late hours, drinking whiskey and telling stories is it?" He and Tommy had done a fair amount of that together. "I know the tale. I'll be playing only the light music myself this year. Pibroch's for younger men."

It was late in the mostly pleasant afternoon by the time Major Forbes' turn came to play the strathspeys, reels and marches. There were other fine pipers in the open class, but old Ben was dominant, and won, along with prize money, a bottle of Glen Fiddich, which he insisted they must take to his hotel room and open with a couple of other friends.

At times Tommy'd been able to lose himself completely in the music and in the sense of living at a different, far-back time of his life. Reality and foreboding would come back in a cyclical sort of way which probably had something to do with the time-release factor in his Dexamils. He decided to save them.

But later, sitting and drinking with the pipers, going out to eat and back to the hotel to drink some more, had a lot of real, not hallucinated, comfort in it. Much of the conversation was piping stories and shop talk, which he hadn't been around since the last contest, and the men were of a kind with whom he felt comfortable, men like family even if they weren't, old warriors, men like Joe.

22

SUNDAY MORNING he was surprised to find that he didn't want to stay to hear the pibrochs. He'd have thought that was his reason for coming. It puzzled him. He didn't think it was because of the foreseen pain of knowing himself to have been the peer of the competitors once, for he'd had no expectation of winning against men who played every day. He was still puzzled when he started the Honda and rode north again.

The men with whom he'd spent the evening were still sleeping, so there were no goodbyes.

He rode to Port Mulgrave, crossed the Canal and was on Cape Breton. He kept on north, up through the granite mountains, past the beautiful seascapes, until, around midday he was at what seemed to be the farthest northeast point of land on the continent. Only the island of Newfoundland lay between him and Scotland now. Had he come because his heart was in the highlands?

He couldn't be sure. He tried to calculate whether he had enough money to quit the music business and move to Scotland. To go gently. That he was able to consider it told him how much calmer he was today than yesterday.

He rode slowly along the mountainside, above the sea, and came to as strange a house as he had ever seen. it was a small, narrow, two-story stone house, disproportionately tall, which leaned a little to the left, in a clearing above the road. The yard was unmowed, and some of the windows broken.

Tommy parked the bike and went up to the house. There was a padlock on the front door. He went back to the road for a better look, and heard young girls' voices.

Two teenagers on bicycles were coming along toward him. When they were close enough he waved them down and asked them, "What is this place?"

"We call it Hippie Joe's castle," one of them said, and they both giggled.

"He was a Yank ran off from that war."

"Vietnam."

"He built the house by hand. Carried every stone up here from the beach."

Tommy looked down. The beach was a couple of hundred yards downhill. It was a hell of a carry.

"Did he live by himself?"

"There was a woman came with him, but she left when he started killing himself."

"I don't understand."

"Starved himself to death, Hippie Joe. It was something to do with an Irish boy in prison, who was on a hunger strike. So Hippie Joe struck with him. They say Joe listened to the radio news, morning and evening, to find out if the strike was still on."

"He was crazy."

Yes.

"He died from it, and they've locked up the house."

Yes, they had.

"Kids think it's haunted."

Maybe it was.

"Nobody knows what to do with it."

Tommy did.

He waved goodbye to the girls, and waited until they were ten or fifteen minutes' gone. He knew he had come to this place to play as much as he could of "Lament for the Children", play it to whatever place in the middle his breath would fail, play it with no listeners except the ghost of Hippie Joe.

He got the bagpipe out and moved up the hillside in front of the house. He checked the beating reeds in the three drones, the double reed in its chamber in the chanter, set the pipes in the stocks and taped the joints.

He put in the blowpipe, and slowly, not calling on his lungs for effort yet, filled the bag. He hit the bag once, to start the sound, and began to play. Somewhere, no

more than halfway through and just as he'd expected, he
ran out of breath. He didn't try to force it. He let the
music sound out, diminish, whisper out over the sea,
and now it was time to start back to whatever word was
waiting for him.

II

1

JOE LEFT the Interstate at the Millinocket exit, drove through town, and stopped at a supermarket on the west edge where he'd shopped on earlier trips. Millinocket was a papermill and lumbering town. It got vacationers in the summer, but there wouldn't be enough of them on hand in May for the store to be stocked up on things like fancy cheese and fresh raspberries. What produce they had was always nice, though, and he liked the butcher.

He got a cart, found fiddleheads and huge artichokes, big firm mushrooms and fragile hydroponic lettuce. He took his time, a man on vacation. He aimed to reach the Pemberton in time to set up and fish the evening rise, but he was going to have a nice fat fiddler to feed, make that a pudgy piper. He hoped the old horse was doing well in the contest, liking his vacation as well as Joe was liking his, and now to see the butcher, who remembered him well:

"Joe the fisherman. My man."

"Enjoy the salmon?" Two years ago on his way to the river, Joe'd learned that this meat cutter was crazy for fresh fish. On the way out Joe'd left him off a couple of nice salmon.

"Whatever else you buy, you're going to find a couple of pounds of filet mignon in the sack."

"Will you grind it for me?" Joe asked. "My brother's a tartare steak freak." That meant buying capers and anchovies. He had the eggs and onions already. He bought

87

a frozen duckling, a fresh turkey breast, and a nice-looking piece of corned beef brisket. He got ribeyes, a couple of big veal chops, and some sour cream and noodles, and then rounded up the breakfast stuff—hot sausage, slab bacon, buttermilk pancake mix and maple syrup. And there'd be trout and salmon to eat. Bet on it, and go back to produce for some fruit.

It would be fun cooking with Tommy, and they could do anything on the little stove in the pop-up camper, anything that didn't take more than two burners at a time.

He bought honey-roasted cashews and smoked almonds to go with drinks, and pushed his shopping cart over to where the store had a display of cassettes. Here he was, carting up a number-one music machine, with a brother coming who'd probably spend a bunch of time lying around camp, playing tapes. There was a cute high school girl browsing there, with a shiney rhinestone barette holding back her light brown hair.

"I need help," Joe said, smiling at her.

She returned the smile. "You buying tapes for your kids?"

"Tell you the truth, I was thinking of serenading some fish." Made her laugh. "Right music might put them in the mood."

"You going up to the river?"

"The west branch. If I don't decide to settle down here."

She laughed again. "It's pretty up there, but the water's awful strong. You be careful." She touched his arm. "What kind of music do your fish like?"

"I think they just like to keep up with whatever's in. Anything you buy, I'll get one, too."

That pleased her, and she quickly picked out three pop tapes, saying, "Here goes my baby-sitting money."

They weren't tapes Joe knew about, except for one country and western group that featured a song called "Diesel Daisy Anderson." The drivers played that one a lot on the jukebox at the truck stop.

But Tommy always kept up with what was popular, and liked just about everything else as well. Along with the pop stuff, Joe put a jazz cassette in his basket, starring Dizzie Gillespie, some big-band swing with real familiar tunes on it, a tape he thought he'd like of a folk singer accompanying herself on the Irish harp, and, at random, a couple of things by Mozart. He'd seen the movie.

"Your fish like all those kinds of music?"

"Makes 'em dance. Out of the water and into the frying pan."

She touched his arm again when he said so long and thanks. It was sweet. So was the slightly older girl at the checkout. Jesus, it was a sweet world, and Joe McKay was going fishing.

2

HE HAD two impulses when he first saw the familiar water of the Pemberton again after two years. One was to speed up and get started. The other was stronger. It was to stop the truck and just go watch the river for a minute, as it passed behind some trees along the road.

His right front tire decided for him. The fucker suddenly started making a noise like sticks across a washboard, and then, as he pulled right, meaning to get out and check it, went all the way flat. So he did get out, looked, and could see a big, ugly, silver nail head sticking out of the black rubber.

"Thanks, pal," Joe said to the nail, and walked away, over to the river's edge, where he stood, leaning against a birch tree, looking down.

God, it was a beautiful river, an awful strong river as the music girl in Millinocket said. It wasn't one of your playful, sparkling rivers. It was a damn serious river.

He watched it moving in the long pool beside which he stood, thinking of the mysterious lives fish lived down there, out of sight, creatures so different they couldn't use the air that kept us alive, anymore than we could use theirs.

He wondered if he could set his music machine to record. He wouldn't mind having a few minutes of the sounds this river made in various places. Here it was a steady, powerful hum. Moving along it, you'd start hearing a throb in the hum. Then, nearer the rapids, it would change to a turbulent growl, and right beside them turn to a good, fierce roar. You could almost fish this river by sound. The salmon liked it rough.

Who talks to rivers? Duckbrain Joe McKay. "Noisy bugger, aren't you?" He said to the West Branch of the Pemberton, so that things wouldn't be too solemn between them.

"Hey." It wasn't the river answering. It was a fairsized, plump-faced young man with a couple of days' growth of beard who'd come up behind Joe. Because of the noisy water, Joe hadn't heard his car stop. "Hey, you've got a flat tire, you know? It's your right front."

"Right," said Joe. "Thanks."

"You knew it?"

"Yes. Thanks anyway."

"Well, aren't you going to change it? Doc and I saw it going by in the car. We were in Millinocket." Up on the road was a big blue Oldsmobile, with Illinois plates, and another man, an older one, behind the wheel, waiting while this young one imparted information. "We wondered if you needed a jack or a lug wrench or anything? We've got all that stuff if you need it. Doc says, when you go camping, be prepared."

"Thanks. I've got what I need."

"Well, how come you're not changing it?"

Joe smiled and shrugged and started away from the river.

"Shit, you want us to help you? We could. I'll bet you want to get started fishing, am I right? You a brother fisherman?"

Joe McKay had dealt with a lot of young men, trained them, had them report to his orderly room as replacements. Automatically, he found himself noting about this one: *Couple of degrees off plumb.* He was the kind Joe and Frank Zimansky, Joe's supply sergeant in the 27th, used to call Silver Stars. The other guys would crap on or avoid this kind of soldier, but he'd be nutty enough to make a hero if the chance came.

"Thanks," Joe told the Silver Star. "I can handle it okay."

"Carl Shumaker is my name. Hey, I'll bet you're Joe McKay."

Joe shook the hand the plump-faced fellow offered. He

looked to be around twenty-five. "Now how in the hell do you know that?"

"That old man at the gate? Old Arnie? He told us about you." The gate, eight or ten miles west, was where the state-owned road ended. After that, the land belonged to a paper company, which had built and now maintained a continuation of the road for hauling out pulp wood. The paper company also leased the campground to a concessionaire. Arnie was gatekeeper and campground manager. "The old man says you're some kind of fisherman. You going to show us how? Hey, did you bring your fish smoker? Can we use it, too?"

"You catching that many fish?" Joe asked, walking back to the truck now, with Carl Shumaker beside him.

"Well, not so many, but we've only been here three days. Hey, Doc. This is Joe McKay. That's my uncle, Doc Miles."

The driver of the Oldsmobile had gotten out of the car. He was another plump-faced man, twenty years or so older than his nephew. He wore steel rims, was clean-shaven, and had a pleasant, droll look about him.

"Hello, Joe," Miles said. "You having trouble?"

"About five minutes' worth. How's the fishing?"

"Spotty. But Arnie says you're the man to catch them."

"I sometimes have a couple to spare for him."

"Doesn't he fish? I mean, imagine, living right here."

"He can't see well enough to tie on a fly anymore, and he gets mad if you go to help him. But he was one of the best. Hell of a bow man, too. We used to run white water."

While they talked Joe'd gotten out his jack and lug wrench, and was ready to put the jack in place.

"Want help with your tire?"

"Thanks. Why don't you guys go catch the evening rise?"

"We've got site 6," Doc Miles said, getting back in his car. "Stop by for a drink. You coming, Carl?"

"Let me take this lug wrench a second." Joe came out from under the truck to see young Shumaker struggling to loosen first one wheel lug, then another.

"Someone must have put these on with an air wrench," Carl said. "Shit, I can't budge the damn things, Joe. Boy, I'd like to get the guy who put these on with an air wrench . . ."

"You start 'em with your foot, Carl," Joe said, and showed him how. It didn't take more than a few minutes longer to change the tire with Carl's help than Joe would've spent doing it by himself.

3

ARNIE WAS in the middle of the road by the gate, grinning, with his arms spread out as if he meant to block the truck, so Joe pretended he was going to run the old bugger down before he stopped short and jumped out.

"Get out of my way, crowbait," he yelled. The blue Olds was stopped just up the road.

" 'Tenshun," Arnie yelled back. "What kind of sorry recruits they sendin' . . ." By which time Joe had grabbed him in a bear hug, but not too strongly. He could feel the fragility of the seventy-two-year-old bones.

"Hey, Top," Arnie said, hugging back. "Where was you this time last year?"

"Getting loose to come fish with you this year," Joe said. "You ready to get in the bow of that canoe?"

Arnie looked up with affection at the scarred canoe riding on top of the truck. "That's our old honey, ain't it?"

"Doesn't work right if you're not in her with me. What do I have to do to get you to go fishing?"

"Hey, Top. Why should I bother when I can send you out to get 'em for me?"

"Negative, Sergeant Clark," Joe said. Arnie had been in the regular army at Pearl Harbor time. "Man in my outfit wants to eat fish, he's got to catch fish." Arnie'd been busted, for some reason. Joe never inquired why.

"Well, you can just turn that truck around," Arnie said. "I ain't opening no gate for some big shot Top Sergeant don't want to feed his troops."

"Well, then. I'm just going to have to take off these stripes and pound you," Joe said, squaring off.

"Watch your ass." Arnie was delighted. He swung, and Joe dropped his guard to let Arnie punch him, chest, diaphragm and shoulders. "Had enough?"

"Hell, yes. You win." Joe said, laughing.

The gate fee was four dollars. The camp site was sixteen a night. Joe paid for six nights and two gate fees. "Second one's for my brother, Tommy. He'll be coming tomorrow or the next day. Let him in, and send him up to 17, okay?"

"Your brother?"

"He'll be on a Honda motorcycle, riding down from Canada."

"One of them bikers?"

"No. He lives in New York. It's easier to park a motor-cycle."

"Can he catch fish?"

"I doubt it. Arnie, shake my hand. I got divorced."

"Don't it make you lonesome?" Arnie's wife had died, four winters back.

"Makes me free to come fishing."

Just then Carl Shumaker arrived, having trotted over from the Oldsmobile, saying: "Everything all right here, guys?"

"Excuse me?"

"We saw you fighting. Hey, Joe, was it about the camp-ing fees? They raised it from last year, huh? Listen, you need some money?" Getting out his wallet.

Joe didn't know whether to hoot or get pissed. He decided to let it go by. "Carl, you don't have as much money as me and Arnie need," he said.

"Ain't that much money in the whole world, son," Arnie agreed. "Hey, move out, Top. Come visit tomor-row noon when it gets too bright to fish."

4

ON THE road between Cape Breton and Pictou, Tommy changed his mind. He'd started back thinking he'd look up the pipe majors for another familiar evening of booze and shop talk, but as he thought more about it, it seemed as if the Tommy who would have relished that might have drifted off with the pipe music over the cliff and into the sea in front of Hippie Joe's castle.

He stopped, took off his helmet, swallowed a Dexie, and let himself grin, thinking of that fat Tommy, swimming into the surf now, on his whale's way to Newfoundland.

Over on the right, although there was no house or lawn, there was a bed of a couple dozen daffodils that must have bloomed that morning, they were so fresh. He got off the bike and went over to them, feeling delight. Leaned down so that he could look at one closely, the six flat petals a paler yellow than the center cone, which stuck up fringed and golden. The day was perfect, calm and clear. The hills, when he straightened and looked up at them, were totally beautiful. It made a man want to bellow.

Tommy McKay put his hands on his hips, threw back his head and bellowed, a great, wordless shout of delight, defiance and despair, all at once. He took a deep breath, and bellowed again, feeling ventilated, and climbed back on the bike.

Just before Pictou, passing the golf course, he started seeing kilts again. There were four who had apparently just come off the course, and flagged down a car for which Tommy had to stop. The men were flushed and laughing as they loaded their golf bags and themselves, tussling over who was going to get to sit in front. When the road cleared and Tommy was able to go around the car, he saw that there was a dark woman driving.

He stopped at a rather fancy restaurant, and liked their lobster Thermidor a lot. He had coffee and a brandy, felt lazy and decided to take a room for the night at a hotel across town from Pictou Park. He wanted to avoid running into anyone he knew, and did, although there was a party of five in the hotel bar where he had a second brandy, who were slightly familiar. It took a minute or two to decide that they were the four kilted golfers and the woman whose car they'd stopped.

She seemed to be Indian, or maybe they said Native Canadian up here.

It was a pretty boisterous party. The men were buying beers, and passing a bottle of whiskey around under the table. Tommy listened in, and gathered that the men were local and the woman a stranger who'd been willing to stop when they waved her down. She seemed not to speak much English, but the men had some French; she laughed a lot and was clearly having a good time.

They were somewhat past medium drunk when Tommy finished his brandy and went up early to bed.

He slept only four or five hours in spite of the Quaalude he'd popped, woke sometime after midnight feeling lively as a reel. It was the best he'd felt since crossing the border. He could see lovely moonlight out the window, and it made him decide to get dressed and ride on a while through the night. He took a Dexic so the mood would last.

5

JOE FOLLOWED the Olds along the road, followed it across the river and downstream along a dirt track off which the camp sites opened. The blue car turned in at site 6. Joe honked goodbye and drove on.

Seventeen was the last site on the north bank. Joe liked it because there'd be no one camped next door on the downstream side. Even better, he saw as he went by that there was no one using 16. In fact, there were only three other sites in use altogether. It was Sunday, might stay this way till the weekend. Thumbs up. Joe didn't care for fishing with company, or camping in a crowd either.

He backed the camper into 17, stopped at a level-enough place, twenty feet up the bank from the water's edge. He unhitched, got in the truck and moved it forward a bit, got out and put down the camper's legs, popped it up and hooked on the door.

Inside, he made his bed, connected the gas and water lines, and got the Coleman lantern out, though it wasn't time to light up yet. He put the perishables in the fridge and poured himself a small bourbon to make the start of the vacation official.

Good. Went out into the fragrant woods downstream, birch and balsam, and picked up kindling with which to start his campfire later. The was a nice pile of firewood by the picnic table. Arnie'd left it for him.

Took the new radio down to the table, turned it on. It pulled Boston loud and clear.

"Believe I'll have another taste of bourbon and string up," he said to himself aloud, companionably, just like he was his own best friend. There was still a long half hour before dark.

Not enough time, though, to lift off the canoe and rig it; just take the truck up to the concrete bridge and walk up along the rapids.

He got in and started, drove past the mostly vacant campsites, feeling how lightly the truck moved without a camper to pull, feeling the same way himself, as if he'd shed his pack and stacked his rifle after a march.

He parked, got out, slipped into the new waders and wading shoes and jointed up the eight-foot Orvis graphite rod he'd built from a kit two years before.

Nice, nice shoes. Thanks for the dee-vorce, Deedee, or I'd never have these nice, nice shoes.

He remembered telling Doc Miles that old Arnie couldn't see well enough to tie on a fly any longer. Joe's eyes were on the way down shit hill, too. Had a small flashlight clipped to his vest, and a pair of reading glasses in the shirt pocket, and needed both to put on a Bomber, a big, brown, Atlantic salmon fly of which he'd tied a dozen for this trip.

There wasn't much wadeable water alongside the rapids. Only here and there could he get out a step or two to cast, and he didn't spend much time doing it. It was more like warming up than fishing.

He was enjoying the noise and rush of the river, and startled to hear voices shouting, indistinctly,

Hang on . . . oh, Man . . . Jesus.

Looked out and saw a couple of yellow rafts tearing along past him, full of hollering young people in wet suits and crash helmets, bouncing off rocks, going through the slicks about ninety-nine miles an hour, having a great time, and it made him grin because it put him in mind of Little Joe.

He'd had great times himself, running this water in a canoe with Arnie, ten, twelve years ago. And goddamn, look at this: Arnie then was the age Joe had just reached, and Joe didn't do white water any more. So Arnie at sixty must have been a damn sight better man than J. McKay was now at sixty, right? Thinking that interesting thought, J. McKay got and missed his first strike.

Idiot. Tenshun, ofuckingkay? What catches fish? Concentration. You know that. Every time you cast, expect a strike. Got it?

Okay. Rule 2. If you get a good strike and miss it, try again, same spot, same lure, a couple of times. No? Okay, Change flies and try the spot again.

He went to a Grey Ghost, a streamer fly that imitated smelt. He wasn't especially fond of fishing streamers, and this one didn't seem to cause much excitement down in salmontown.

How about a, let's see, Wulff-tied, light grey Adams? Sure. Let's get back to fishing dry.

The Adams didn't do any better than the Ghost. Next rule: after trying other stuff for five minutes, go back to the fly you got your first strike on.

He did it, made his cast, and the moment the Bomber touched water, the fish struck again, and Joe hooked him. Damn good fish, too, but he was on for only a couple of seconds. Dived into that strong current and snapped off Joe's fly and leader, come on, fish, you're acting like you don't want to get caught, cleaned, skinned and eaten, for some reason. Bringing up the next rule: a fish with a sore mouth forgets he's hungry. Move along.

Joe moved along.

At the head of the rapids was a big salmon pool called The Wilbourn, where Joe caught his first fish, though he knew as soon as he hooked it that it wasn't a salmon. It didn't have that kind of power. It took the big Bomber almost delicately, made a short run, turned toward the fisherman for a single, pretty leap—a nice, eleven-inch brook trout.

Joe waded out and used his net to land it, though he could easily have beached the fish. But he enjoyed the tug of the current against his thighs, liked knowing he had supper in hand. It would soon be dusk. Time to amble back.

Time to have a big, slow drink. Time to clean the fish. Time to cook it, enjoy it, pour another drink, build a fire, and sit comfortably at the picnic table on the riverbank with his radio ballgame.

These things would be easy and pleasant, and he was letting his mouth water and his gut yawn for the big, slow one, when he went by site 16 and saw a GMAC, 4-wheel-drive wagon with huge, silly tires pulled in there. Its lights were on when Joe drove past, and the Jimmy-wagon's driver could be heard opening, then closing his door as Joe got out of the pickup. The driver was coming over to 17, through the trees.

"Hey, Joe. Joe McKay. Did you get a fish? Can I see it?" It was the Silver Star himself, Carl Shumaker.

Joe hesitated, shrugged, and said, "Hello, Carl. Just a brookie."

"Let's see."

"In the creel," Joe said. He'd left the creel, landing net and fishing vest on the pickup seat, and was getting out of his waders. The door of the truck was open, the courtesy light on. Carl picked up the creel, opened it and handled Joe's brook trout.

"Oh. One of these," he said. "Hell, we throw these back."

"You're not as hungry as I am," Joe said.

"You want to see my rifle? It's a Mauser, and I sporterized it myself. It's in the wagon. Let me get it."

"Not tonight," Joe said.

"In the morning? See, I'm more of a hunter than a fisherman. You like to hunt deer?"

"Not me," Joe said. Being in the New England woods with ten thousand happy triggers wasn't Joe McKay's idea of fun. He liked to hunt wild turkeys, alone in the spring, when there weren't many people out.

"I was thinking. I'm next door to Doc and my Dad. You see their trailer? It's pretty neat, but I sleep in the wagon. I could get my stuff and move up to right where it's parked now. I believe I'll do just that."

"My brother's coming in tomorrow," Joe said. "I was kind of hoping 16 would stay open so we could spill over into it."

"Your brother?"

"Yes."

"Hey, that's great, but listen, I'll pay for it. Let me pay for 16, so nobody else will show up and take it."

"You're quite a man with the money," Joe said.

"Listen, what I came for. We're going to drive to Millinockett, there's this bar with TV, to watch the Celtics. You want to come?"

"No thanks," Joe said. "You guys go ahead."

"Come on. It'll be great. We'll have some drinks, and it's a great bar. It oughta be a great game, Huh? Don't you watch basketball?"

"I'll hear it on the radio."

"Yeah, but on TV . . ."

"Carl," Joe said. "I'm a hungry man. I want to get organized now and cook supper."

"Want me to help? I'm a good cook."

"No, kiddo. I want you to take off, now. Could you do that for me?"

"Oh, sure. Okay, Joe. You want some peace? Okay. Okay, I'll see you, right?"

"I guess you will," Joe said.

6

HE'D BUILT his fire, found his game, and mixed an after-dinner drink, when Carl showed up again, but not alone. His uncle, Doc Miles, was with him, and so was John Shumaker, Carl's father. John was married to Doc Miles' sister. Got that, Joe? Want to turn off the radio, just as the game gets started, so they can make this information absolutely clear? Sure you don't want to drink their bourbon instead of yours?

("Well, it all smells like dog piss," Joe said. "I'll just walk my own pooch.")

Also along, to join the party Joe McKay seemed to be giving, contributing a case of beer and lots of wonderful noise, were Brad and Grady, a couple of lean country boys from Pennsylvania who'd migrated to Pittsburgh and become steel workers. Only when the mills closed down, they went into construction, and probably Joe ought to turn off the game a little while so he could enjoy that information, too. Brad and Grady were intemperately for the Bucks, and don't make any goddamn mistake about that, sergeant. They hated the horseshit Celts. Brad and Grady were camped at 5, next door to the Miles-Shumaker bunch.

"What happened to your television trip?" Joe asked.

Aw, it got late, they said. And they'd got to drinking, and Joe had this swell radio, Carl told them. Was it all right? Carl said Joe'd probably like some company.

What Joe considered saying was, why don't you borrow the radio, and I'll do some sleeping? Or, let's take the radio down to your end, because I might want to slip off early? But the game had started, and Bird was having a fantastic night already for the Celts, so what Joe did was let them stay and drink and yell, sitting around the rugged picnic table by the river, radio in the middle, while he loaded up on a little more dog piss than he'd quite meant to, and concentrated as best he could on hearing the game.

Boston won it, 111 to 98. Bird had forty points. Grady got pretty put out, and Brad, who was drunker, said that Bird oughta be hung up by the balls.

"He'd still make ninety percent of his free throws, upside down," Joe said, and Carl Shumaker laughed so hard at that he got the hiccups.

7

MAYBE THE strangest thing that happened to Tommy, on his strange trip to Canada, took place in the dark hours of Monday morning, after he'd left the hotel to ride in the moonlight.

To give his dumb head something to do as he rode along, Tommy started thinking through a new arrangement of "Molly and Tenbrooks," which would give his new mandolin man a solo. He just about had it figured out when he saw that he was coming up on a disabled car with its headlights on. It was in the ditch beside the road, rear end down. The driver must have lost control, hit the brakes hard, spun and slewed in backward.

The car was resting on its oil pan and drive shaft, and would have to be towed out. Tommy stopped, thinking the driver must be still inside, though he couldn't see anyone. He walked over to the car and looked in the window. The front seat was empty. The back was empty, too.

The car seemed familiar, though he didn't see how it could be. It was a big, old car, a long, brown-and-yellow Thunderbird, with bent fenders and rust spots. Tommy reached in the open window and turned the headlights off. Probably the driver'd gone for help and been too rattled to think about his battery running down.

Then, half a mile along, going through a wooded area, Tommy saw what turned out to be the driver, a woman with black hair and blood on her face, trying to scramble into hiding in the bushes along the road. Tommy stopped again.

"Are you all right?" he called. When there was no answer, he called out again: "Can I do something to help?"

The woman rose slowly out of the bushes, and Tommy saw that she was the Indian who'd been with the golfers in Pictou.

"Not cop?"

"No. You've hurt yourself."

"I wreck car." She came up onto the road and walked toward him.

"I saw that."

"Cut my head."

"Let's look at it."

He got off and beckoned her around to the front of the motorcycle, where he could look at the cut in the light. She'd been thrown sideways, apparently, when the car bottomed out, and hit her head on the dash, or maybe the righthand door. There was a gash, but not a deep one, and some bruised tissue around it. It had stopped bleeding.

"Let me get my first-aid kit," Tommy said.

"Get? You not speak French?"

"Bandages," Tommy said, and went around to the luggage carrier, where he kept the kit and a thermos of black coffee.

He poured a cup of it and took it to her.

"Here. Drink some of this," he said. She started laughing. "Funny coffee?"

"Making me sober?"

As she said it, he could smell the liquor on her breath, and realized she must have left her car in fear of a cop coming along and finding her in it, drunk. He handed her the cup, and used some more of the coffee from the thermos to wet a gauze sponge.

"Sorry, no water," he said.

"Someone like you help someone like me," she said in a disbelieving way, and turned up her forehead to let him sponge it.

"Why? Because you're Indian?"

"White people don't like."

"I like." Tommy finished cleaning the wound and put Mercurochrome and a bandaid on the cut. It was hard to tell the woman's age—she could be anything from thirty to fifty. She was quite handsome in a lean, hard way. She was wearing jeans and a very old sweater, over a tan man's work shirt. "My great grandmother was Indian," he said.

"Huh?"

"Me." He pointed to himself. "Little bit Indian, too."

"No." She laughed again, and then, quite flirtatiously: "You got drink?"

"Yes," Tommy said. "Matter of fact." There was half a bottle of Scotch left in the back of the trailer. "Coffee first, okay?"

She frowned at the cup she was holding, and then poured it out on the ground, and Tommy's hallucination was getting cranked up again, intensified by the pills he'd taken and the Scotch they shared: he was with his great grandmother that night.

It began as a kind of joking with himself, as she told him she'd been on her way from Cape Breton to see her sister in a town called Axton, and stopped off in Pictou because four funny men in skirts had flagged her down just before she reached town.

Sounded like Great Granny all right. She'd got herself

flagged down by a kilt, hadn't she? The fugitive from Scotland who married her, the probable assassin, was a wild man, and his roguish wife some kind of outcast from her tribe. Now she'd flagged Tommy down, was his to protect, and damned if she didn't seem to expect it of him.

Those golfers who stopped her were plenty fun, and one she liked too much and was in the car with her, into the woods with whiskey for a little while.

She'd come down from Cape Breton that day because her home had been foreclosed. She had nothing but the car and a few things in the trunk of it. Could he be her great grandchild? Sure, he could. Hop on, dear.

He'd never had anyone ride behind before who held on so tightly. Could it be because she lived in a world of horses and wagons—come on, fat guy, let's not get silly. But he rode slowly because she was scared, and it took nearly half an hour to reach Axton that way. Then, when they came to the shack where she thought her sister lived, the door was locked and there was no one home.

It was an unpaved, unlighted street they stood on, though the moon was bright enough so that they cast shadows.

"Indian street," she said, her bandage showing white in the moonlight.

"Been here before?"

"One time. Four year."

Though it was past three in the morning, there were lights showing in one of the other shacks. They walked to it, and Tommy said, "Maybe they know when your sister's coming back."

She hung onto his arm so that he'd go to the door with

her. Tommy did the knocking. A woman's voice yelled
something in French. Tommy's transubstantial passenger called back, saying her name probably, and there
was a moment's silence, then a stream of what was cer-
tainly abuse as the speaker came toward the door.

"Come." Great grandmother was pulling urgently at
Tommy's arm. "I know who. She don't like me."

Tommy let himself be pulled away.

"Four year time her husband sweet on me."

They got as far back as the sister's possible shack
before he saw a giant Indian woman open the door to the
lighted shack, who continued to shriek at them in extremely unmusical French. She was not somebody
Tommy felt like arguing with about his G. Granny's outcast honor.

They went back to the motorcycle.

"Where we go?"

"I don't know," Tommy said. He couldn't take her
along with him, a thought which brought with it a wonderful image of doing just that, and showing up at Joe's
fishing camp, saying "Look who I found and brought
along." He couldn't possibly leave her. "Let's go back to
your car. You have things in it."

"Cop come."

"I'll stay with you till morning," Tommy said. "If the
cops come, I'll talk to them. In the morning we'll come
back here, and I'll hire a tow truck to get your car out."

She was scared on the way back, and cold.

He dozed through the rest of the night, sitting with her
in the front seat of the battered Thunderbird, under a
blanket he got out of his trailer. Sharing it. He kept a
protective arm around her shoulders. It was a while

before she stopped trembling, and Tommy did not understand nor need to understand why comforting her was of such comfort to himself.

8

THE DAY after Bird scored forty points Joe caught three fine salmon large enough to keep, and threw back more smaller ones than he bothered to count.

There was a light hatch of some kind on the river when he woke up and went down to the water to wash his face, pleased and surprised that he had no hangover. His back was stiff and his knees wobbled, but hell, that was every morning's report from the interior. There was mist rising from the water, and salmon and trout appeared in it here and there, breaking up through the surface, feeding on the hatch. Close to where he stood he could see insects of some kind, a cloud of them, hovering, falling onto the surface. He slipped off his pants and waded into the cold water to scoop one of the little guys into his hand.

Back up in the camper he lit the lantern, put on his glasses and took a close look at what had got the fish excited. He couldn't name it, but it had a gray body and brown wings, and was about a size ten. He got out a fly box he hadn't expected to use, hadn't even carried it yesterday, and in one compartment were some flies he'd tied the year before for a different fishing trip. They were dries, but he couldn't recall the name.

They were eights and fourteens, but the gray and brown color match was pretty good, and he didn't want to stop now to get out his kit and tie tens.

With a hatch on, and he hoped hard it would last till he got launched, he'd do best fishing smooth water. He dressed warm, had a fast coffee, and hauled ass, chewing on a glazed doughnut that tasted wonderful, to the Wilbourn, at the tail of which he'd caught last night's supper.

He parked off the road, with about thirty feet of steep footpath between him and a place to put the canoe in. Unfastened the old girl, and maneuvered her onto his shoulders, staggered a step or two until he got his stupid knees lined up right, and carried the lady down the bank, grinning at the idea that she'd put on weight. Rigged the anchor, got the fifty-pound hunk of concrete with *Arnie* painted on it out of the truck, for weight in the bow. Strung his rod, put it in the boat, shipped a paddle and was on the river before sunrise.

The mist was still hanging. The hatch was still hatching. Which got him excited. All it took, though, was one stroke out into the current for Joe to get cautious. Even here, a hundred yards above the rapids, the river could take control and move him downstream, fast and helpless, especially with no one in the bow.

"All right, big balls," he said to the rushing water, and sliced the boat through, angling upstream, adjusting with each stroke to the flow so that it couldn't turn him broadside.

He reached a place where the fish were rising, and

released the anchor. Then he kept paddling until the anchor caught and held, the anchor line was taut and the canoe stopped moving. He laid down the paddle and picked up the rod he'd rigged on shore.

Two small ducks sped by overhead in the mist.

Joe cast the gray-and-brown fly upstream, short, and saw it go by him, quickly, underwater. Retrieved, dried it off, and soaked it in dope to make it float.

He cast again and liked the way it rode now. Retrieved and made his first long cast, out to the right, watched the line move away, couldn't really see the fly, but, knowing where it was, did see a fish hit it. He struck, and had it hooked. Felt and pranced like a pretty good salmon out there. Joe got excited again, but he played it carefully. It took about five minutes to work the fish in close enough to net, and Joe knew by then that it was too small. Fourteen inches was the legal keeping size, and this little salmon wouldn't make eleven.

"Okay, buster," Joe told it, wetting his hand and then lifting the fish out so that he could remove the hook. "You were fighting out of your weight class." He slid it back into the river and watched it flash once and disappear.

He caught and released three more small salmon before he saw one swirl at his fly that was clearly legal, but the wiseass wouldn't take. When that happened again, twice, though Joe continued to catch and release small fish, it was time for even a slowbrain fisherman to ponder.

The fly was right, the hatch still on, and the fish feeding. These larger, smarter buggers must be seeing his leader at the last instant, and scooting off. Joe reeled in, broke off the fly, got out some two-pound-test material and tied a couple of feet of it onto his leader for a tippet. He'd had a nice fish break off a two-pound rig last night, but that was in much rougher water. Better to fish light, get a keeper on and try to ease it in than never have it take the fly at all.

End of ponder. Time to change position.

He weighed anchor, guided the canoe in a fast drift over toward the north bank, and let the anchor down again. A couple of minutes and two small fish later, his judgement paid off. There was a smashing hit just as the flyline straightened out downstream, after a long float. Joe didn't have to strike. The fish hooked itself hard, and Joe imagined it had been chasing the fly for ten or fifteen feet.

He let line run off the reel, thumbing it lightly, until it was down to the backing, and he was glad he had plenty. The fish took off forty yards of backing on its first run. When it ended, Joe did some really tight-assed stripping in, moving the fish upstream toward himself and got maybe twenty of the yards of backing into the boat before the fish dashed off again. This time Joe thumbed a little harder, and so they went at it, the fish running, Joe thumbing, Joe stripping in, and the fish running again for however long it took. A man concentrating that way isn't counting minutes.

Almost abruptly, the salmon got tired. Joe got his backing in, and a good bit of the line before the final run, and not too much of it went out again. He turned the fish and started gentling it toward the canoe, until he could see it, making little nervous darts back and forth under the surface. He got his landing net under the fish and lifted it out. It was a male. His mouth had started to beak.

"Wow," said Joe, out loud and with admiration. "You are one noble sonofabitching salmon." He'd go eighteen inches and over two pounds. Joe moved the net and the fish over the center of the boat, got a finger into the gills, stunned him with the back of his closed clasp knife, opened the knife and gutted the fish. A noble sonofabitching supper for Tom McKay.

He sat up and relaxed for a moment, looking around him at the riverbanks. Then he realized there was something puzzling going on, looked again, more steadily, at the north bank, and caught, as he moved his eyes along, a glint of sunlight bouncing off glass. Kept staring at it, until it moved and turned out to be a pair of binoculars. And then, maybe because he could see he'd been detected, out stepped Carl Shumaker, waving.

He must have been there, hiding and watching, as Joe caught his fish.

The hatch was still on, but Joe McKay wasn't on the west branch of the Pemberton to provide spectator sport. He ignored Carl, pulled up his anchor, and paddled toward the south. Then he thought, *Oh, shit, you know the poothead doesn't have social instincts,* so he looked back over his shoulder and returned Carl's wave.

He moved down to a pool called the Big Zigg, just below the bridge, where he fished standing on a big smooth rock in a ferocious current that moved straight toward him, so that when he got his second keeper it was running straight at him and he was able to use its own momentum to flip it out and onto the rock beside him. He glanced at the bridge to see if Carl had moved down to watch some more, but there was no one there.

It was a lovely day, Joe was hungry, and two was the legal limit of fish.

He got his equipment stowed away in the truck and drove east, stopping a little way up the road from Arnie's trailer. He walked toward it quietly, and then around the side, peering out to watch the old buzzard dozing in a deck chair in the sun. The pale blue eyes winked open, though, when Joe tried to sneak up and lay a salmon in Arnie's lap.

"Gotcha. Don't take another step." Arnie had Joe covered with a Coke bottle.

"What else have you got?" Joe asked. "Anything like a sharp knife?"

"If I didn't dull it shaving this morning," Arnie said, got up, went inside the trailer and came out with a fileting knife and a cutting board. "You got me something to clean?"

"No. Got me something to filet," Joe said, reaching for the knife and board. He put the board on top of a sawed-off stump, put the smaller fish on it and made Arnie hold and admire the larger one while Joe slabbed off the meat from the sides of the other, turned each slab and sliced away the skin. He did the second fish, laid the four filets side by side, and said: "Take all you want."

"This looks like lunch." Arnie picked up one of the smaller pieces.

"You can use the other one, too."

"I don't have that big appetite any more," Arnie said. "Thanks, Top."

"Don't suppose my brother's come through yet?"

"I'm watching for him. Hey, I looked for you on my

morning walk. Where was you fishing?"

"I was by the bridge later on. On those big rocks on the south bank where the current turns."

"Always liked it there. Caught me some good fish there. Guess by the time you hit 'er, I was turned around and walking home."

9

JOE ATE the other small filet for lunch. Then he rubbed his two big filets with salt, pepper and garlic salt, set up his smoker, lighted a small green-wood fire, and hung the filets inside where they'd take about five hours to cure.

It was cool, but it was sunny. He put one of the foam mattresses from the camper down outdoors, got his sleeping bag unrolled on it, and slept a while. When he woke he got out a maul and a tire iron, and worked up a sweat repairing yesterday's flat. It was a while since he'd had to work a tire off a wheel rim by hand.

The paper company had a little store with a gas pump a couple of miles up the road. He drove up there, bought a Snickers bar, asked about an air hose and learned they didn't have one. There wasn't one any closer than Millinockett, but Joe carried a cylinder of compressed air with enough to inflate a couple of tires, so he was okay for now.

At the store he was above the rapids which fed the Welbourn, near a pool called the Little Zigg, which, for some reason, he'd never fished. He drove to it, launched the canoe and learned the water here was extremely deep. Since no fish were rising, he decided to experiment with a new fly, copied from one another fisherman had showed him two years ago. Damn thing looked more like a cigarette than a trout fly—a long cylinder of deer hair which he'd flared, trimmed and lacquered white. It had a red stripe down each side and a little bunch of malibou feathers for a tail.

It was meant to imitate smelt, and the guy who'd showed it to Joe had salmon he'd caught on it to show as well.

It was odd: salmon and smelt were both sea-running fish, born in fresh water, returning to it to spawn—but landlocked, here and in a few other places, both species together for reasons biologists couldn't agree on. Anyway, salt or fresh, smelt were the salmon's favorite food. There were times when the paper company opened the dam at the head of the river, and pieces of smelt came through, chopped up by the turbines, along with whole fish, and the salmon started acting like sharks.

Joe fished the imitation smelt, which floated under the surface in a deep part of the Little Zigg. Rubber boats went by. A white-water kyack went by. Hell of a good way to get wet. As Joe watched it go, something took a tremendous yank at his smelt fly and broke it off, and what was that first rule, McKay, you dumb fuck?

He tied on a duplicate, changed position, and caught his third keeper of the day. He was glad he and Arnie had eaten the smaller salmon already so that he still had a legal possession limit, unless the warden came after them with a stomach pump.

It was evening now, and he thought Tommy might have arrived. He put up his gear and drove back to camp, but Tommy wasn't there.

Carl Shumaker was, though, and damned if the silver asshole hadn't moved his truck and stuff into site 16, after all.

Carl was, in fact, sitting at fucking Joe's picnic table, drinking beer with his friends Brad and Grady, playing fucking Joe's radio, and looking hungrily at the salmon in the smoker.

"Hey, Joe," Carl called out. "I watched you catch that fish this morning. I wish I had a movie of it. You were great."

Joe nodded. "Listen, guys," he said. "When I got divorced, earlier this year, my wife said I was getting to be lousy company. She was right."

"Hey, listen," Carl said, in a voice inflected very much like Joe McKay's. "You got no business fixing anything that smells this good, if you don't want animals coming in out of the woods."

"Here." Joe unhitched the screen on the front of his smoker, and lifted out one of the filets. "Take it and clear out, will you? I want to take a bath."

Carl took the fish. Brad grabbed it from him and ran a couple steps, while Grady held Carl back. Carl cursed. The other two laughed, and they all cleared out, the construction workers more or less tossing Carl up into the driver's seat of his own wagon.

10

TOMMY DIDN'T come that evening. In the morning, before he started fishing, Joe went down to the gate to tell Arnie where he planned to be.

On the way back from that visit, he saw Carl, Brad and Grady off in the woods to the left, more or less across the road from Joe's campsite, and slowed to see what the three fearless mouseketurds were doing this time. The fearless ones appeared to be looking at an orange oil drum on wheels, which was all right with Joe, who turned into his camp to get his fishing gear.

"Hey, hey Joe. Come look."

Umm-hmmm. Ran all the way, didn't he?

"Come on. It's a bear trap."

"Any bears in it?"

"Come on. I'll show you how it works. I figured it out."

Oh, well. Joe grinned and went along. He wasn't getting a sunrise start this morning anyway.

"Hey," one of the construction men said. Joe couldn't remember this morning which was Brad and which was Grady. "Look at this mother."

The mother was indeed a big oil drum, painted orange, with both ends cut away. On its side was painted, sure enough, DANGER, BEAR TRAP, and Carl didn't really deserve to be congratulated for figuring out its operation. The far end had a steel grid welded across it, just inside which was a device to hold bait. A steel cable ran through overhead pulleys to a latch at the open end.

When a hungry bear climbed in and started to munch on the bait, the bait-holder would act as a trigger, pulling back the cable to release the latch, and a steel door on tracks would clang down past the animal's rump like a guillotine blade. It would lock automatically.

"What do you think of it, Joe?" Carl asked. "Shit, that's a strong trap."

"Haven't we all made box-traps like it?" Joe asked. "For coons and rabbits in the garden?"

"Just kids do that. I'll bet nobody ever caught a real rabbit that way."

"My father did," Joe said. "Till I got big enough to take over."

"Think these guys catch any bears?"

"Sure they do, and haul their butts away from the camping area, and turn them loose, I'll bet." That was Brad's bet if it wasn't Grady's.

"Hey, I wish they wouldn't," said Carl. "I want to see a bear."

"If you do, be nice to him," Joe suggested. "There isn't anything you can do that a bear can't do better, including run, swim and climb a tree."

"How about shoot a rifle? Listen, Joe, say no if you want to, but it won't hurt to ask, huh? Can I go fishing with you in the canoe? Shit, it would be so great to watch you catch one, like yesterday, but up close."

"Wait a goddamn minute." Joe decided it must be Brad, giving the order. "If somebody's going in the canoe, it oughta be a man who can catch fish."

"Yeah." Grady took Carl from behind with a mild choke hold, and started giving him a Dutch rub. "Brad and me can flip. You didn't take this piece of chickenshit to raise, did you?"

"Turn him loose," Joe said, raising pieces of chicken-shit having been his true and holy vocation. "Let's go out for an hour or two, Carl."

As he said it a picture came into his head of a stretch downstream that was smooth with no rapids for a good mile. It was a pretty safe stretch, and he'd caught salmon there.

"I know. Sure. Hey, thanks. Let's, but I know you don't want to stay out too long." When Carl got excited, he couldn't stop talking. "You're watching out for your brother. I don't blame you. Hey, it's the second game tonight, right? Shit, I hope Tommy gets here in time for the second game with us. You want to go to Millinocket if he does? Hey, Joe, all we've got is spinning rods. You going to teach me to fly fish?"

"Not from a canoe. When I show you how to cast with a fly rod, we'll be standing in the water. Your spinning rod'll get 'em, buddy."

11

WHEN THEY stopped at site 5 so that Carl could get his rod, John Shumaker, Carl's father, came out of the trailer, smiling. He was a small guy who looked physically tough, and wore the same kind of steel-rimmed glasses as his brother-in-law Doc Miles. Shumaker was a retired corn and soybean farmer who held out his hand to Joe while Carl was gone.

"I just want to thank you," Shumaker said. "For taking an interest in my boy."

It was a little embarrassing. "It's okay, John," Joe said. What the hell else could he say? How about, *bullshit, John, take him off my back.*

"He needs someone like you. To look up to, to help him get right."

"I don't know," Joe said. "I don't mind Carl." A really delicious *bon mot* there, from *The Collected Wit and Wisdom of Joe McKay,* right?

Carl had declared himself more hunter than fisherman, and he wouldn't have had to be a very damn good hunter to make that statement true. Once they were on the water, he didn't seem to understand his spinning tackle well enough to cast his lure to the same place twice, and he retrieved so fast it would have taken a fish reduced to idiocy by hunger to believe the white Rapala was moving under its own power.

After a while, though, Joe got wanky-brain to slow his retrieves enough so that Carl started catching small salmon, every one of which he wanted to keep. "Not in my canoe, Sport," Joe had to tell him.

"Hey, come on. I want to show those guys."

"You don't listen so good, do you? I said not in my canoe."

"They think I'm chickenshit."

"They couldn't be right, could they? Come on, let's get you one," Joe said, and, in time, he did, hooking a fish that felt plenty big enough on the next-to-last of his bombers. He handed Carl the rod. "Keep the tip up," he said. "Let him take some line." And talked Marmaduke Monkeydong through thumbing and stripping till the fish was in the net, a nice sixteen-incher. He showed Carl how to kill and gut it, gave him the fish, and pulled anchor.

"Shit, we're not going in when they're starting to bite? Joe, we can get more like this, maybe even bigger, shit, let's stay thirty minutes more, you want to?"

"No, Carl," Joe said. "Now you've landed one with a fly rod, we go in and I show you how to cast with it."

If Carl Shumaker could catch a keeping-size land-locked salmon by himself on a flyrod, it would do him more good than any interest in him Joe McKay might take.

Back at camp, Joe said, "Put your waders on," and got into his own. Then Joe jointed up the spare fly rod, tied on his last Bomber and gave it to Carl along with a box of flies. He left the young man up to his ass in water, practicing fly-casting, an idiot skill at which Carl actually caught on pretty quick. As for Joe, he made himself a sandwich and took off, wanting a change of scene and company.

He drove into the huge wilderness of Baxter State Park, parked, followed a footpath, located a pretty stream to wade, and spent a soothing afternoon catching and releasing brook trout. One of the things that made it soothing was the complete absence of human voices, unless you wanted to count his half of the conversation between Dr. Doolittle McKay and Mama Moose.

She came browsing along the edge of the stream, followed by her calf a couple of hours after Joe started fishing. He saw her upstream, first, in a place where the bank was clear, moving slowly into sight, her pendulous muzzle swinging. By the time she was hidden again by alders, the calf was in the clear space, shorter and smaller, of course, than his mother, but with such long legs that you wanted to cheer every step it took without falling forward on its chin.

Then it was out of sight and in a moment the mother was in view again, practically at Joe's side where he stood in shallow water, a bulky, dreamy-eyed animal who seemed totally tame.

"Hello," Joe said. "Looks like you had a good time in the moose yard last winter. First kid?"

The moose yard was wonderful. We tramped snow.

"That a boy or a girl?"

Seen any willows? I'm hungry for willow shoots.

"Downstream, about half a mile."

Goodbye.

"Goodbye. Hello, junior."

The young'un was too shy to talk, or maybe hadn't learned yet.

Bootleggers used to ride moose in the time of prohibition, back and forth across the Canadian border, nothing could move through woods and swamp like a moose, and where the hell was Tommy?

Back at the paper company's gate, he asked Arnie that question. Arnie shook his head. Joe could only suppose Tommy hadn't caught the right moose yet.

12

DURING THE second game between the Celtics and the Bucks, Joe's all-time favorite useless player, Bill Walton, reinjured his ankle. Walton had hurt himself so often through the years that he was never a real factor in the NBA, but he was still a pretty damn thrilling player to watch. Joe'd seen him once in person, playing off-season with an all-pro team in the the summer of '80 against the American college stars who were going to the Olympics. It was an exhibition game, a fund-raiser, and Joe couldn't have said any longer who won.

What he did remember clearly was Walton's dominance in the few minutes he played. All those guys were larger than life, but the big redhead dwarfed them. Even away from the ball, you watched Walton, couldn't keep your eyes off him.

Tonight, with Carl Shumaker celebrating his now-famous fish and the rest of the sporting characters on hand as before, Walton had come off the bench for the Celtics and was contributing when he went down.

Joe groaned. "My man. Shit, fellows, that's my man. Got everything he needs on earth except some better way of connecting his legs to his big, long feet."

"I hope he hurt it good," said gracious Grady.

"Me too, the son of a bitch." Brad, from whom all blessings flowed.

The closing minutes of the game were tense, and when the Celtics won it, 126-124, the cursing of the construction men over the crackling fire and noisy radio was loud and furious.

"Turn that fucker off before I bash it with a bottle," Brad said, and turned it off himself. Grady gave young Carl Shumaker, who was crowing for the Celts, a backhand shot on the upper arm that half knocked Carl down. Carl's father, John, went to his boy. Carl's Uncle, Doc Miles, stood up to Grady. Joe sat still and watched the fire. And Tommy McKay appeared silently in the firelight, just up hill of the picnic table.

Stood still there, with the light playing on his face, looking at Joe. There was something about him that made Joe unable to do anything for a moment but stare back.

Carl, getting himself straight, spoke right out, though: "Hey, look. Is it Tommy?"

"This your brother, Joe?" John Shumaker asked.

It broke the trance. "Goddamn right," Joe shouted, jumping up, and pushing through the group to give his brother a hug. "Tommy, you pisshead, you're late, damn you." He squeezed. Tommy squeezed back. "What'd you do, walk all the way, pushing your dumb motorcycle? Shit, I better show you how to start the thing sometime. God, I'm glad to see you."

"Hello, Joe. I've been sitting by the camper, waiting for your game to end."

"We didn't hear the bike."

"You've got noisy friends."

He seemed tired. Generally old Tom would have been in the middle of things by now, shaking hands and making jokes and laughing. And the firelight should have made his cheeks look ruddier. There was some kind of pallor there.

"Damn." Joe hit him lightly in the stomach. "You lose a couple of pounds?"

Tommy laughed, and kind of shook himself. "Hope so. Hey, basketball fans."

"Hi, Tommy." Carl was first, of course. "Come on. Have a drink. You like bourbon?"

"Thanks. I've been drinking Scotch."

"Where's your bottle? Let me pour you one."

"It's up by the camper." Tommy was accepting other introductions. It wasn't in him, Joe knew, to be anything less than the gladdest hand in town in a situation like this, no matter how tired from a long, bumpy motorcycle ride the man might be.

"This series isn't over yet, guys," he was saying to Brad and Grady. "Wait'll your Bucks get 'em in Milwaukee."

"Be a damn different story," Grady said.

"We're gonna put it to 'em," Brad agreed.

Then Carl burst back onto the scene, said he couldn't find Tommy's Scotch, come on, have a bourbon, how about a beer, and hey, did Tommy win the contest? Tommy drank, and said he sure as sweet and hot did not, those boys in skirts weren't going to let some Yank walk off with one little nickel's worth of prize money. Scotch from the tops of their heads to the tips of their dicks.

After that, Brad and Grady said goodnight quite cheerfully and left. Doc Miles and John Shumaker stayed for a little more sociability, while Carl spun and scrambled till his Uncle suggested that the McKay boys might like to have a chance to talk.

As soon as they were gone, Tommy deflated and said, "Let's sit down."

"Tell me about your contest, buddy," Joe said. Tommy sat on the picnic table bench on the side away from the fire. Joe sat on the table top. "You couldn't score this time?"

"I didn't play," Tommy said. "Two days before I went up. At Little Joe's school, as a matter of fact. I learned I wouldn't be able to cut it on the pipe."

"Why not?"

"I'd have run out of breath."

"Come on. You've got lungs like a walrus."

Tommy shook his head. "Not anymore."

"Well. I guess it creeps up on all of us," Joe said. "How's our boy?"

"No."

The flat way he said it made Joe shiver. "Tommy?"

"I don't like telling you what being short of wind means in my world these days."

"No, Tom."

First one, then the other of Tommy's elbows went up on the table top. The hands became fists, went together, and the forehead pressed against the thumbs of them. Joe felt something he'd never expected to feel again. It was quite particular: you'd sent out a patrol. They got into a fire fight. Now they're sifting back into the company area, sitting down here and there, exhausted, and the patrol leader is moving toward you to tell you who isn't coming back. "No, Tommy."

The hands went down. The eyes looked across the table. "It's one of the early symptoms," Tommy said.

"Where do we go to get you tested?"

"It's been done. In Cambridge last weekend. Heard the results day before yesterday. Had to get examined some more. That's what made me late. I've got it, Joe, the fairy-killer. God who loves us found a way to slap the

wrists of bad little fairy boys, only the way he slaps, it
breaks off your hand and the rest of you goes pouring
out the stump. What's the dirty new four-letter word?"

By the time he'd finished speaking, Joe was down beside him with an arm around Tommy's shoulders.
"AIDS? What are we going to do about it, Tom?"

Tommy didn't answer right away. A stick of wood in
the fire blazed up and died back. The river noise that
Joe'd got used to seemed very loud again.

Joe said: "How sure is the test?"

"Pretty sure, but we did others to make certain. What
makes you short of breath so you decide you've got to get
tested is PCP. It's a kind of pneumonia. Maybe you know
all this?"

"Read about it. But go on."

"There's a drug called AZT. Hasn't the alphabet got
ugly? Anyway, I'm on AZT, so I feel okay. But if you test
positive for AIDS, and you've already got this PCP, the
barn door's open and you're not going to see the horses
anymore."

Then Tommy reached across and gave the back of
Joe's right hand a squeeze, and said: "Hell, I'm sorry
about coming on like the goddamn muse of tragedy. I've
given the matter my best thought the last couple of days,
as you might imagine. There's no way I'm different from
a guy's got terminal cancer. Terminal anything. Everybody's got to pay the fiddler, and there's nothing in the
book says the jolly fiddler doesn't have to pay, too."

"All right, Tom."

"The only difference between you and us terminals is
that we know what's going to get us, and more or less
when. If somebody doesn't squish me under a truck or

drown me in the river first, I've got about three years. That's a lot of time, Joe."

"How can you know when?"

"Statistics. Nighty-eight percent are off the beach within three years after it's diagnosed."

"There can be a cure in three years. There's an army of people working on it."

"Couple of squads. Joe, I know how you feel about the President. No matter what sorry specimen's in there, he's your commander-in-chief. I just wish Wrinkle Dick and Nancy didn't take the same attitude as God who loves us. Hey, Little Joe's okay. I had a hell of a good time with him. Best ever."

"I'm sorry you couldn't play the 'Lament.' It was going to be for the friends you've lost, wasn't it?"

"Yeah, Joe." He paused. "Yeah. Bruno. Fletcher. Gary. I wanted the audience to mourn them with me, even if they didn't know they were doing it."

"Tommy, what are we going to do? I asked you that before."

"Right away?"

"Right away and after. Both. You don't want to stay here, do you? Let's load your bike on the pickup and drive back to my place. You'll be a lot more comfortable."

"The camper looks comfortable. I think I'm going to like it here." Tommy stood up. "I like the way the river sounds and the woods smell."

Joe stood up, too. "Okay, we stay. But think about moving in with me in Connecticut when we leave. I've got a lot of room now Deedee's ass is out of the way. You don't need to work, Tom. I'm making good money, and

I get damn lonesome. It would do me good to have you around."

"We'll talk about stuff like that tomorrow. After you catch me a salmon for breakfast."

They were strolling slowly up the bank now, toward the camper.

"Your salmon's already smoked and ready."

"I want a fresh one for lunch. You're not going to wriggle out of going fishing."

Headlights came on at site 16, and the sound came of Carl's GMAC wagon starting up and driving off.

"Basketball fan?" Tommy asked.

"Carl. The nutty one, but it looks like he's got a good heart. I told him I'd like that site vacant while you're here."

"It's cold enough to frost tonight," Tommy said.

13

JOE'S GUESS at why there was a vacancy at site 16 was as wrong as Tommy's supersmart brother could be.

He and Joe were eating this delicious smoked salmon and eggs, warm in down jackets by the fire, playing a little Top 40, when Carl Shumaker's father, Tommy didn't recall the first name, appeared on the bank above them.

"Joe?"

"Morning, John. You want some breakfast?"

"Joe, I got a scared boy down there this morning."

"Why do you call Carl a boy?" Joe asked. "He's twenty-six. If you'd treat him like a man, he might just make one someday."

"Joe." The little man seemed to be ignoring Tommy. He hadn't shaved yet, and seemed to have the shakes. "Joe. Carl needs to know if your brother used the outhouse when he came in last night."

"Mr. Shumaker," Tommy said. "I can promise you, if you got off a motorcycle after four hours' riding, you would definitely use the outhouse. Now what is this?"

"He heard you."

"Heard what?" Joe sounded a little cross.

"Heard you talking about it. Your brother's got AIDS. Carl went to the outhouse. Then he was bringing your brother a bottle of scotch from his wagon, and he heard both of you." The voice trembled. The words spilled out as they did when this guy's son talked, tumbled over each other. Oh, Jesus.

"Oh, Jesus." Education time. "Mr. Shumaker, you can't get AIDS from a toilet seat."

"Carl said you drank from his bottle. And we all shook your hand."

"But my hand wasn't bleeding, I'm happy to say. I'm not bleeding anywhere, Mr. Shumaker. There's no way any of you folks could have got infected."

"That's not what Dr. Miles says."

It was a real effort for Tommy to suppress his opinion of Dr. Miles' opinion.

Joe said: "Looks like we better have a talk with the doctor."

"I have some literature to give him," Tommy said, which might help unless Miles was a total dyslexic. Tommy'd known a doctor or two who seemed to be.

"You want to meet with us? He said, tell you to meet with us."

"So why didn't he come with you?" Joe asked. First-rate question, in Tommy's view, though the answer was obvious as a mouse on the dinner table. The kindly old practitioner was avoiding the area of contamination.

"Where does he propose to have this meeting?" Tommy asked, and then, double-checking that mouse: "At your camp?"

"No sir. In between."

Joe said: "We'll be at the picnic table at site 9 at 8:15."

"You be there," John Shumaker said. "Or you can pack your stuff and leave out."

As he turned to go, Tommy couldn't help laughing. "Aren't you supposed to salute the man, Joe?"

"What's wrong with us?" Joe said. "We haven't even been standing at attention."

They heated water from the river and washed their breakfast dishes.

"Is that right, Tommy? About the blood?"

"That and other body fluids I didn't think I needed to mention under the circumstances. You didn't know how this cruddy thing gets transmitted?"

"We hear all sorts of junk."

"You'd better read the literature, too."

"I want to."

"It's a lazy goddamn virus, AIDS. It only gets into your bloodstream where the skin's broken. Or with a needle."

"Okay."

"You didn't know that for sure, but you didn't hesitate to hug me."

"Come on, peckerbrain. If there was any reason not to, you'd have said so. Let's put the sleeping bags out in this cold damn sunshine."

14

BY EIGHT o'clock it was warm enough for Tom to take his jacket off. By noon, it might be hot. God, what a wonderful place. You could have all four seasons in a single day.

They started walking up along the river, which was one awesome-looking body of dark and dangerous water.

"You really take a canoe out in that?"

"This is the tail-end of some rapids that come out of a big pool by the bridge," Joe said. "I used to run 'em. Don't any more. Where I fish from the canoe, it's pools and flat stretches. Want to go out after we see these jerk-offs?"

"I'm as close as I want to get to that water now," Tommy said. "I think what I'd like to do is take a nap in this gorgeous place."

"Didn't do much sleeping in Nova Scotia?" They turned away from the river, and walked the dirt road. The walking was easier.

"I was doing Dexamils. You've got to see Nova Scotia,

Joe. Especially Cape Breton. It's exciting country."

"Even without Dexamils?" Joe poked him one. Tommy biffed him back. "Maybe we can go back up there later on this summer. There's Atlantic salmon fishing there."

Tommy told him about Hippie Joe's castle, but not about playing the bagpipe there. He'd save that. And the story about family-hallucinating. Great-grandmother. Tommy had some stories.

They reached site 9 and sat down at its picnic table. And along came a nifty blue Oldsmobile.

"This'll be our pals," Joe said.

Doc Miles and John Shumaker got out.

"Hello," Joe said, and indicated the bench on the other side of the table.

Miles hesitated, like he thought maybe the AIDS virus could ride over and up his pantleg on the morning breeze. Then he slid in opposite. John Shumaker stood behind Miles, glaring through his glasses. "There's kind of a panic on, fellows," Miles said.

"That right?" Joe was doing the talking for now. Tommy figured it was best to let him.

"Carl's been drinking ever since he got up," John Shumaker said. "I tried to get him to stop, and he said, 'Keep away from me, Dad. Don't touch me or you'll get it, too.' And ran off into the bushes."

"The boys from Pennsylvania are packed up, talking about leaving," Miles said.

"There's no need for that," Joe said. "Can't you convince them there's no need for that?"

Miles didn't answer.

"Have you treated any AIDS patients, doctor?"

"No, sir."

"But you've read the medical literature?"

"In my part of Illinois there are so few cases . . . No, I haven't read up on it. I do understand that it's a highly infectious disease, with one hundred percent fatalities."

"Wouldn't a doctor need to find out about it, just in case?" Joe asked. "Just to keep up?"

Miles ducked that one, swam underwater for a while and came up spewing out a lovely, simple request: "I asked for this meeting to make a simple request," he said. "We'd like you to leave. We have a boy on our hands who's capable of being quite deranged. If you'll go, I think we can handle him. If you're unwilling, then I'm prepared to call the management of the paper company."

"What are you prepared to tell them?" Joe asked.

"The exact situation."

Joe rose up: "How in the hell can you tell them the exact situation when you don't know what the fuck it is, doctor?"

There was a brief silence, and then John Shumaker sort of squeaked: "They could be liable."

"Liable to laugh in your stupid faces," Joe said, looking like a man about to take violent action, which was good because if he was Mutt, now it was time for Tommy to be Jeff.

"Shush a minute, Joe," Tommy said, and got out the pamphlet he'd been carrying in his shirt pocket. He'd picked it up, and a couple more like it, in Boston. "If you want to tell anyone the exact situation, this will tell you what it is. It's a pamphlet about AIDS and how it's transmitted. It doesn't pull any punches. It's in layman's language, doctor, but it's scientifically accurate, and I think you'll find it reassuring."

Miles didn't reach for it. John Shumaker said, "Joe, won't you consider leaving here?"

"You've got a son that thinks he's infected," Joe said. "That booklet will tell you that he can't be. If the doctor won't read it, put on a pair of fucking gloves and read it yourself, John."

Tommy said to Miles: "You think you're at risk if you touch this thing?"

"I simply don't know. As I've just finished saying."

"Where did you learn your medicine?" Tommy asked.

"In Iowa, if it's any of your business."

"Davenport, Iowa?"

"All right. I'm a chiropractor. I didn't claim to be anything else."

"He's a first-rate chiropractor, too," John Shumaker said.

He looked to Tom McKay, the soul of patience and understanding, like a first-rate vomit brain. The soul said: "May I read you a short section from this booklet? About how AIDS is transmitted?" Neither man replied. The soul, putting as much dramatic expression into it as he could manage without laughing, began to read aloud. It took about three minutes, and was real clear stuff. He put the booklet down, and said: "Okay, gentlemen. Do you think you can calm some people down? Seems like they listen to you, Dr. Miles."

No answer.

Joe, who had walked away angrily and been staring at the river, swung around and walked back. "Here's the deal," he said, in a voice that added: *no backtalk.* "You read the booklet. You gather in the ding dongs and give 'em the information. If you can't get the message over, let us know, and we'll clear out. But you're going to have to show me that you've read and understood. Got it?"

Miles finally broke silence. "Who wrote that?" He asked.

"An AIDS support group," Tommy told him. "They're tough people. They have to be. I picked it up in Boston to give Joe."

"Let me think about it," Miles said, whatever that meant, but Tommy was on his feet, alarmed.

"Joe?"

"What? Yeah, I smell it, too."

"Smoke."

15

JOE SWUNG out of site 9 and ran up the road. He couldn't see where the fire was, but the wind from downstream was full of the smoke and he called back, "Let's go", and was nearly knocked down by some asshole in a speeding car going the other way.

For a guy who'd anchored his high school relay team, Joe McKay was one slow piece of constipated camel shit. His back and his knees slowed him down. But his lungs were in shape, unlike poor Tommy's, and Joe was able to keep jogging. Going past site 12 he could see that the smoke was localized. It was dark gray, almost black smoke.

Through the trees at site 15 he could see that it was his camper burning, damn it, had he left something on the

stove, left the goddamn stove turned on? The camper
looked swollen up, inflated.

Another forty yards and he could see it starting to
dissolve. The plywood subfloor was going, the bunk sup-
ports in flames, the vinyl top melting down, aluminum
ready to go. As he ran to it, the glass in the door shat-
tered, and he had hot glass shards in his face, but it gave
him a glimpse of the cabinets burning away inside, and
he knew there'd be nothing to salvage.

No frozen duck, no turkey breast, no veal steaks. No
extra fly boxes, no fridge. The gas tank exploded on the
side away from him, doing no extra damage.

By the time Tommy arrived, walking, breathing hard,
the flames had already started to die down. The steel
frame and the wheels were all that was going to be left.

"Son of a mule-fucking bitch," Joe said. "Did I leave
something on the stove?"

Tommy said, "Joe?" Then he kicked at an empty gas
can. "Is this yours?"

"No. It sure isn't."

"Somebody wanted us out of here bad."

Joe looked at the gas can, picked it up, and threw it as
far as he could, yelling, "Grady and pusballs. Let's go."

He climbed into his pickup. Tommy climbed fast into
the passenger side. "It must of been them that nearly hit
you on the road." Doors slammed, and they jolted off.

"Joe," Tommy said. "If we catch them, can we handle
the bastards?"

"Shit no. They're young and strong." He and Tom
would have to equalize.

"Turn back, then. I've got a gun in the Honda tool
box."

"You?"

"It was Mom's."

"Don't tempt me." Joe swung the truck into the road and went fast.

"What's the plan?"

"Demolition derby. I'm gonna ram their car till they haven't got a car."

16

AT SITE 5 they slowed down. It was empty. "Looks like they didn't stop," Joe said, and drove on fast, across the bridge and down to the gate. Arnie was in the middle of the road, flagging them down. Joe braked so hard the truck stalled, and yelled out the window:

"Those Pennsylvania scumbags go by here?"

Arnie ran up. "Yeah. Hundred miles an hour and didn't pay."

Joe started the truck back up. "I'm going a hundred and fifty then."

Arnie grabbed the edge of the truck window opening.

"Hey, wait, Top. Calm down."

"Turn loose. Those cuntheads burned my camper."

"You just ain't fast enough, Top. Let the cops. They burned her?"

"Goddamn their sons and daughters. What cops?"

"State troopers. I already phoned it in about them not paying. Now, you come in the trailer and we'll call again, and tell the cops what else."

"He's right, Joe," Tommy said.

"Fuck it, I guess he is," Joe said, turned off the ignition, sighed, smiled and got out. "I'm supposed to be the cool head around here, but I am absolutely wrong and you gentlemen are absolutely right."

"They oughta get 'em right before Millinocket," Arnie said. "Except for Baxter, there ain't no place for them to turn off, and I already talked to the guy on the gate at Baxter. Only other thing they could do is turn around and come back here."

"Old as I am, I don't think they better do that," Joe said.

"Turn the truck around while I make the call," Arnie said. "I want to see that camper."

When he got back, the righthand door was open and waiting. Arnie said, ready to climb in: "Didn't get much look at you last night, Tommy. Don't much resemble your brother, do you?"

Tommy smiled and slid over toward Joe, who said:

"Wait, Arnie. Tell me something before you get in. Have you heard about AIDS?"

"Like nurses' aides?"

"No. It's a disease. It's killing off a lot of people. Tommy's got it."

"Godalmighty, son. I'm sorry to hear that."

"You sure you want to ride with us?"

"Well, he can't give it to me, can he? Notice you're riding with him." Arnie got in and closed the door. "Is it hurting you, Tommy?"

"No. I feel pretty good, thanks."

"Glad for that, anyhow, and I'll tell you. Whatever's

gonna kill a man my age, he's already got inside him, sure as hell."

"That makes two of us, then," Tommy said, and smiled back.

The camper was still smoking when they got there. The blue Oldsmobile was parked at site 16. Doc Miles and John Shumaker were walking away from the gutted camper toward their car.

Miles stopped and turned toward them. "Joe," he said. "I'm really sorry this had to happen."

"Sure you are," Joe said.

"Joe, your car insurance is going to cover the camper," It was Shumaker.

"Yeah."

"Have you seen Carl?"

"No. I haven't seen fucking Carl."

"Doc read that pamphlet Tommy left. He wants to tell Carl things are okay, not to worry. The boy's out of his head."

"Is there anything we can do?" Miles started to walk over.

"You can fuck off," Joe McKay suggested.

17

THEY'D TAKEN out their sleeping bags to air that morning, and the foam pads, too.

"We've still got something to sleep on," Tommy said. "And I've got a mountaineer tent." It was in the trailer, attached to his motorcycle, now parked at the edge of the clearing. "Not to mention a bagpipe, a clarinet and a fiddle."

"Are you proposing that we stay another night?" Joe asked. "And maybe throw a musicale?"

"It's your fishing trip," Tommy said. "We can stay if you'd like to."

"I got anything you want to borrow," Arnie said. "Dishes and pots. Got a Coleman stove."

"But the food burned up," Joe said.

"Look." Tommy saw something that could make a man smile. "That's the bottle of Scotch I was drinking from while I waited for the game to end. Would someone like a drink?"

"Hell, yes," Arnie said.

Tommy picked up the bottle and handed it to Arnie. Arnie had a pull and handed it to Joe. Joe had a pull, and gave it back to Tommy. Tommy had a pull. Yeah.

"Well," Joe said. "I'll admit that makes me feel better. And I might just catch a salmon, and we can get canned stuff at the company store. But, no. I don't want to spend another night here. Let's eat that last piece of salmon in the smoker and think about moving out."

"No," Tommy said, pleased but not wanting to show it. He didn't want to retreat in some kind of pissy little panic, either. "Let's eat the salmon in the smoker, and you go fish a while."

"Now you're talking," Arnie said.

"Jesus," said Joe. "That's the second time I am absolutely wrong and you fuckheads are absolutely right."

But he didn't sound as sure about it as he had the first time around.

18

JOE OFFERED again to take Tommy with him in the canoe. Tommy said he wasn't that crazy. He'd take his Scotch bottle, and sleeping bag, and have a nap near the river—but not too near. It was about ten-thirty now. He'd probably sleep till noon.

"Let me see that little gun Mom gave you," Joe said.

"Sure." Tommy went over to the Honda and unlocked the tool box. What he came back with was a .25 caliber, pearlhandled automatic, which Joe recognized immediately though it must have been forty-five years since he'd last seen it. Joe took it, hefted it. It practically disappeared in a hand as big as his.

"Lemme see, Top," Arnie said, and took possession. "Yep. What they used to call a ladies' gun. Guys bought 'em for their wives back in that Depression."

"There were a lot of hungry bums around," Joe remembered. "Mom used to keep this in the glove compartment, but I'm sure she never fired it except when Dad made her practice."

"She gave it to me when I went to New Orleans," Tommy said. "She thought it was a rough place, and it was, but I never fired the gun, either."

"Where was I?" Joe asked.

"It was after Korea. You must have been in Germany."

"You really never shot this toy?"

Tommy shook his head. "No. I once threatened a young fellow with it. Otherwise, nothing but oiled it now and then."

"Let's see if it still works. Got ammo?"

"Just what's in the clip."

Joe checked the slide. It ejected okay. He took out the clip and checked to make sure there was nothing stopping up the barrel, reloaded and handed it to Tommy. "There's two safeties," he said. "This thing on top that pushes forward. Forward is off. And this bar at the back of the grip. If you're not squeezing it, the gun won't fire. Here." He handed it to Tommy. "Wait."

He trotted over to where he'd thrown the scumbags' gas can, picked it up and set it on a stump about six feet from where Tommy stood. "Blow a hole in the fucker."

Tommy held the gun out and fired without trying to aim and, for a wonder, hit the can. "Hey," he said. "Thats fun."

"Don't waste another round now," Joe said. "Just tuck the little lady under your pillow when you go to sleep. We'll buy a box of shells when we go down, and practice up." Then he said he'd run Arnie home, and fish where Tommy could find him, see him and signal if anything came up. He'd be in the canoe on the Big Zigg, which was upstream a little way. All Tommy'd need to do was ride his bike up and onto the bridge and look downstream, and there'd be Joe, hooked into the biggest smelt-sucking salmon he ever had on a line, and mad as hell at Tommy for distracting him, okay?

He dropped Arnie off, and drove back to the parking place on the south bank he'd had in mind. It was just off the road in a little clearing. It was a fairly long carry, then, to get the canoe down to the water, and he had the usual fun with his knees. Even after they seemed to be lined up under the weight and he'd taken a dozen steps, the right knee wanted to be favored. "You stupid bastard," he told it. "Stop wobbling." He rested it by leaning the boat against a tree trunk without taking it down from his shoulders.

He went on, the right knee behaving itself now, but with a tremor or two in the slightly less stupid left one. Finally, though, everything seemed to get into balance and he came out of the woods onto a rock ledge he'd been aiming for, feeling better, though his face still stung here and there from the shower of hot glass he'd taken, and what kind of towel do you use after a shower like that one?

It was late in the morning for fishing. When he got the boat out and anchored, he decided to go straight to the smelt fly, even though it was more like an ultralight lure than it was like conventional flies. He also wondered what the hell he was going to do with a fish if he caught one, since he'd about decided he and Tommy ought to head out as soon as his brother got rested. Normally it would have been fine to have a fish to take home, or give to the nice Millinocket butcher, Normally he would have had a refrigerator to transport fish in, not a gaping metal box with its insulation and wiring melted down.

He thought about what he'd do if some insurance money did come in. Maybe buy a travel trailer next time, or even make the down payment on an RV, something to provide a little readier comfort if he and Tommy felt like taking some trips. Then he thought of a trip for both of them to take, which would mean not using the bucks for a vehicle, but for a couple of airline tickets to Scotland and a stay at a nice hotel, or a country inn there. Tommy loved the place. Joe'd gone only once, during the big war, when he was stationed in England, waiting for D-day, and had got a pass. He'd had the feeling of a place he'd love sometime; for now the pipers he'd hoped to hear were off with their regiments, of course, and the streets of the towns and cities dark at night.

By the time he got into that recollection, the rhythm of fishing had taken over, though he still wasn't concentrating well.

Nevertheless, the small salmon were hitting often enough to keep him awake, and thanks to that, Joe found himself, about 11:30, into a very good fish. It could be a twenty incher this time, his biggest yet, which, he decided, Arnie might want. He also decided as he played the fish that he'd leave the smoker with Arnie. It was weird to decide that, look over at the rock ledge, and see Arnie himself, standing there and waving . . .

Joe netted the fish and held it up by the gills to show off, grinning, but how silly, Arnie couldn't see. He said into the noise of the river, "You old fucker. Can't you wait for me to bring this down to you?" Killed the fish, pulled the anchor, and paddled.

Strangely, Arnie never stopped his waving, and when Joe got close enough to see his old friend's features, he realized it was frantic waving, not a greeting.

He gave a big thrust, steered in, and Arnie grabbed the bow and pulled the canoe halfway out of the water. "Joe, go look at your truck."

"Holy horseshit, they haven't burned my truck now?"

Joe pushed himself up and out of the boat, and was on the rocks and running.

"Your tires. All the air's let out."

"Hang onto the boat," Joe called back, and ran up the steep, stony path to where he'd parked, and there it was, clean as cowpiss, his red Chevy pickup hunkered down on four flats, with the valve stems lying around on the ground where someone'd dropped them. Joe gathered them, and put them in the truck on the floor beside the brake pedal.

Then he walked rather slowly back to where Arnie was holding the canoe, trying to figure this one out.

"This morning they wanted to run us off," he said to Arnie.

"Yep."

"Seems like they got scared as soon as they did it and ran off themselves."

"Or they was going anyway, and burnt it for meanness."

Joe nodded. "But whoever let the frigging air out doesn't want us to run off. Seems like they want to keep us from leaving."

"Don't make sense," Arnie said. "Those sorry cocksuckers are too crazy to do anything that makes sense."

"Wait. Not keep us from leaving. Hell, no. Could it be to keep me from getting over to Tommy?"

"Shitfire, Top. Could be, couldn't it?"

"Let's pull this boat up. I'm going across the bridge on four rims."

"There's a damn sight faster way," Arnie said, hanging onto the boat to keep Joe from moving it.

"Arnie?"

"You heard me, Top."

"You sure?"

"You get ready or I'm jumping in the bow and taking her down without you."

"Goddamn, you mean it, don't you?"

"This stretch? We always called it easy."

"Tallyho, goddamnit. Let's move out."

"We can do her." Arnie was grinning with excitement.

"Let me get you the bow paddle."

"What do you think I got right here?" Arnie said. "Turn this boat around and let me in."

In less than a minute they were underway, slanting across the Big Zigg. Joe was remembering now. They'd have to paddle hard to get to where the current reversed, going up the pool. Then they'd fight down and across it, until it reversed again, and go with it along the north bank into the rapids.

"Shout out when you want me to hit it," Arnie called back. "Can't see a goddamn thing three feet away. Just barely see the water."

"Straight and hard for now," Joe yelled back, and then, when they reached what seemed like the right place near the north bank, "Hard right."

They hooked into the current, and as soon as it began to move them it was as if something had lifted the canoe up and was sailing it through the air like a paper airplane. "Here we go, Top," Arnie yelled, feeling it.

"Hard left," Joe shouted back, and they were past the first small rocks, and headed toward a big one over which the water swooped, smooth, treacherous and tumbling on the downstream side.

"Left again." Joe dug his own paddle in, correcting, as

they whipped past the first haystack and bore down on another.

"Give me a stroke," he called, and they evaded it, turned perilously, almost broadside, and Joe yelled, "Let me have it," and dug savagely again to correct, saw where the V was, the place beyond the rock where the divided current met again, and steered into it.

He'd half-forgotten how much he loved this battle with the river.

Going into the next V, they took a hard whack from a submerged log jammed under the rock they were passing. He slid them past it, and shouted, "Hold off," so he could turn the bucking boat diagonally back until it pointed east again, downriver. Then for a moment he could use his paddle just to steer before they hit a strech of shallower water where they couldn't avoid taking a few bumps on the bottom.

Then it deepened and seem to speed up, and they went sleighriding down toward the next haystack. Joe took a fast bearing on the bank and decided this rock was the one that had a short channel just below it. Got into the V, found the channel and steered some more.

"Now left," he yelled, to stay out of new shallow water, but they did scrape, tilt, ship water, and had to paddle hard together to get the boat back into deeper stuff, and then back, the other way, so they wouldn't miss their landing point.

"Turning left now, ready to beach." They kept paddling hard together, hit a rock he couldn't see, almost capsized, shipping more water, and came out into where it was suddenly smooth and swift and safe again.

"Let's run it up," he called, seeing them not far above

site 17, turned just a little sharper than he should have
and damn near scuttled the boat. Safe, hell, he thought,
correcting, and grinning because now they really were
all right, though the boat was wallowing as they headed
for shore.

"You okay, Arnie?"

"Ain't had a wetter ass or more fun in ten years," Arnie
called back, and, with a couple more strokes, the bow
touched shore, ran up a little way, and Arnie was out,
spry as a chipmunk for seventy-two, and Joe himself
went over the side and up to his knees to give the canoe
a big push and help beach it.

Then he did a quick slosh up the bank to where
Tommy'd settled down to nap an hour or so before. The
sleeping bag was empty. There was some Scotch left in
the bottle. The pillow was several feet away on the
ground, and there was no sign of the .25 caliber, pearlhandled, automatic pistol.

"Don't mean something's wrong. Man can take a
walk."

"Yes, a man can do that." Joe said, shucking off his
fishing vest, thinking irrelevantly that the last salmon
must have washed out of the boat, and probably his
landing net as well.

"Want to scout around? I'll sit here quiet."

"Look." It was Tommy's motorcycle. "Oh, shit, Arnie."
Two more flat tires, but these had holes in them. They'd
been shot.

"Goddamn, I'm stupid," Joe said. "Thinking it was the
Pennsylvania pricks. It's Squirrel-Shit Carl and his deer
rifle. You stay, Arnie." For the third time that morning,
Joe Knees McKay was running hard. What the fuck were

they doing? Training him for the geriatric marathon?

Up to the end of the camp site road he ran, and there it was, Squirrel Shit's big GMAC wagon with the great big tires pulled part way into the woods. If Joe'd had a gun he might have felt like shooting a tire or two himself, but what he felt more like doing was keeping very quiet, stalking, and staying out of sight.

The river was on the right, the campsites behind. That left two directions in which to move, downstream along the river, or left into deeper woods.

What Joe was trying to imagine now was Tommy, armed with his little lady's gun, trying to evade and maybe get the drop on a nut with a rifle. The smart thing would be to go left, into deeper cover, where you could move with some concealment and the lanes of fire would be more cluttered. With patience you might find a hiding place that would work as an ambush and hold still there until the nut got real, real close.

But Joe doubted Tommy knew how to think that way, and it might be more in line with instinct to go straight and keep the river in sight to keep from getting lost.

While he was still balancing these choices, two shots decided for him. They were a sharp crack, and a small pop, from straight ahead. The boys were downriver. And no one was dead yet.

Joe dropped to one knee, looked carefully in a quarter-circle, wishing his binoculars hadn't burned up. Then he moved in a crouch for twenty yards, with his face down, dropped and looked the quarter-circle again. The fourth time he moved that way he caught sight of Carl Shumaker kneeling beside a tree, using the trunk for a rest as he sighted his rifle. Joe moved very cautiously now

from tree to tree, and, halfway to his quarry, heard another shot and a man yell out in pain. It wasn't Carl.

Useless anger took Joe's breath, followed by useful
cold loathing. He saw Carl rise and start moving to another tree, apparently looking for a clear shot he'd never
get to take. One hundred ninety-five pounds of Joe
McKay landed on the young man's back, an arm choked
him, and a blow from another arm sent the rifle flying.

Now it was Carl yelling, breaking away from the
choke hold, and Joe grabbed an ankle, tripped the crazy
bastard down, landed on the small of his back with both
knees, jumped up and started kicking ribs. He thought
he heard one break, but it wasn't punishing Carl that
mattered, it was getting to Tommy.

Joe pivoted away and grabbed the rifle. Carl was mo-
bile enough, still, to get his feet under him and come up
with a gravity knife. Joe heard himself give a yell, and
lunged in under the knife hand, driving the rifle barrel
into Carl's diaphragm as if it had a bayonet on it, with-
drawing, spinning the gun down and around to deliver
a good strong butt stroke to the balls, and Carl went
down writhing. A good kick in the head and another to
the point of the jaw stopped the movement, and Joe
stood over Carl Shumaker for a moment, not quite wanting to kill the miserable thing. Joe picked up the knife,
held the blade flat between his foot and the ground,
snapped off the blade and threw both it and the handle
into the woods. Then he picked up Carl's deer rifle and
smashed the barrel against a birch tree as hard as he
could, snapping off the front sight and bending the barrel a little. Reversed it and smashed the tip of the butt
against the same tree so that it split away along the grain,

giving him a sharp walnut stake and a useless barrel and receiver to drop. Then he kicked jaw one more time and ran to where his brother was calling.

Tommy had rolled behind a log. He was pale, shuddering and somehow shapeless. The shot had got him through the right ankle. There was a lot of blood on the ground.

"Joe. God, Joe." He heaved himself onto his back.

"Easy now, babe."

"God it hurts."

"Sure it does." Joe knelt and looked at the wound. "Gotta get your shoe and sock off," he said.

"Don't get blood on you."

"Don't worry." He was getting some blood on him, of course, but he had no wound or sore on his hand, and he wasn't going to worry, either.

He rolled the sock off, and saw the blood pulsing out of the hole in Tommy's ankle. Tommy had an elastic webbing belt holding up his chinos. Joe got the belt off, turned up the right pant leg, found the pressure point and used the belt for a tourniquet.

"Dr. Joe." Tommy was gritting his teeth, with his lips open. The teeth looked very white. The blue eyes were squinted, and there was a lot of leaf mould on the shoulders of the plaid shirt. Joe wiped it off, knowing that his brother was hurting worse and worse all the time. But the pulse of blood stopped now.

"Tommy, I got nothing for pain but Tylenol, and it's in my truck across the river."

"Some in the bike. In my toilet kit. Jesus, will it help?"

"Not enough, probably. Can you walk if I help you?" He raised Tommy to a sitting position, put his hands into his brother's armpit from behind and tried to get him standing. What was the line? *He's not heavy, he's my brother?* Joe McKay's brother was heavy as a fucking hippo.

Tommy screamed. Joe had to let him down again.

"I've got to get some morphine or something," Joe said. "Then maybe we can hop you on one leg. I've got to make sure the nut is out of business, too. Can you bite it till I get back?"

He saw the pearl handled automatic and picked it up.

"No more shells," Tommy said.

Joe put it in his pocket. "Hang tough."

"Joe, your face. Where the glass got you. Don't wipe your face till your hands are clean."

Joe grunted. Wiping his face was just what he'd been about to do. Wiped his hands hard on his pants instead. "In about five minutes loosen up the tourniquet, let it bleed a minute and then tighten up again. Can you do it?"

"Yeah." Moaned. "When you come back, there's gloves in my bike trailer. It's not locked."

Back where Joe had left him, Carl Shumaker was sitting up groggily now, holding what was probably a well-fractured rib. Joe was the armed man now. He had the sharp walnut stake he'd broken off Carl's rifle stock.

Carl said. "Goddamn. Ow. Where's my deer rifle?"

"It's a bear rifle now, bear," Joe said, poking Carl's shoulder with the sharp point. "Get up."

"Quit."

Joe kicked him in the vicinity of the broken rib and said, "Up."

Carl groaned and said, "Quit," and crawled away a step or two.

Joe's belt came off, became a noose slipped over the young man's head and tightened around his neck. Holding the end of the belt while Carl tried fruitlessly to loosen the noose, Joe poked again with the stake and said, "Get up, bear." Prodded the man to his feet, pulling upward on the belt.

"What's this bear shit . . . ow. Hey." Carl was walking. "Hey, you wouldn't. Joe. You wouldn't."

"Faster," Joe said. "Walk faster." He kept the belt half-tight, so that Carl, who had his thumbs hooked under it, couldn't get it off. He kept the stake in the small of the man's back, with pretty good pressure on it, and walked him to the road and down it. The bear trap was in the woods opposite site 17. When they got there, Joe called out:

"Arnie. Arnie, over here."

Arnie appeared on the road. "What happened?"

"This one shot Tommy in the ankle."

"What is he, crazy?"

"Seems to be."

"Tommy all right?"

"We got the bleeding stopped."

"What are we gonna do with the crazy?"

"Put him in the bear trap. Bring the tent rope from Tommy's trailer, okay?"

"Joe. Please. Please."

Joe kicked him hard in the ass. "I oughta kill you, boy, and I just might." As he said it it occurred to him that he could have done Carl a lot more damage, and hadn't. He'd done no more than was necessary to control the idiot.

"It's your brother who's killing us all," Carl said. "Don't you realize? He's the one you oughta lock up, Joe, he's got me infected. I know he does. Probably you, too."

"Shut up," Joe said. Arnie arrived. "Make a noose for his neck. Let me get my belt back."

With the rope noose in place, Joe prodded Carl along to the rear of the orange-colored barrel. Keeping pressure on with the stake, he tossed the end of the rope through the center of the barrel so that Arnie could grab it from the other end. "Pull tight, Arnie," he said. "Be careful it doesn't trip the bait holder."

"Gotcha, Top," Arnie said. "Okay."

The rope was tight. Joe let go of the small section he'd held to maintain control and said, "Keep it tight and low. I need his head down." Pushed the head down and forward, into the trap.

"Bastards, bastards," Carl was sobbing. "Quit. Let me alone. I don't care what you do to me, I'm not getting in . . ." But his chin was already on the metal rim, and all Joe needed to do was grab him around the ankles, lift and shove while Arnie hauled on the rope.

When they had Carl well inside, Joe said, "Okay, Arnie. Trip that thing," and the door clanged down and locked. "Let him take the rope off. Carl, you belong in a goddamned asylum, but this will have to do for now."

They moved away from the babble of obscenities and sobbing, Arnie coiling the rope. Joe's brother was a killer, Carl was crying, infected, someone help. Dad. Someone. Please help.

Joe scrubbed his hands with soap and river water. Then he opened Tommy's trailer, found the gloves, which seemed to be a good idea, and a first-aid kit. With Arnie following, he trotted back to where Tommy was lying.

"How's it going, scout?"

"Great," Tommy got out. "If you like being shot in the ankle."

Joe knelt down and released the tourniquet, hoping the bleeding had stopped, but it hadn't. He tightened up the tourniquet, bandaged the wound and gave Tommy four Tylenols. The pain seemed to be a little less, but Tommy was out of breath from it.

"Arnie, don't get blood on you," he said. "Stay with him. I'm going to see if I can get some morphine."

He ran back to where Carl's wagon was parked and got lucky. The keys were in it.

He got in, started it and drove to site 6, where Doc Miles' trailer was. He knocked loud on the door with the palm of his hand. Miles opened the door with John Shumaker behind him.

Shumaker said: "Have you seen Carl?"

"I sure have," Joe said. "Your son's shot Tommy in the ankle. I've got to get my brother out of the woods and I need some morphine."

"Carl did what?"

"I've got some Demerol," Miles said. "Not that I'd like the word to get around. It works like morphine. I'll go get it, Joe."

He turned and went to the rear of the trailer.

"Where's Carl?"

"Out of harm's way," Joe said.

"Where?"

"I put him in the bear trap," Joe said. "He isn't hurt except maybe for a busted rib."

"We've got to get him out."

"The trap's locked. You'll have to call the Ranger for the key."

Miles returned with a hypodermic and a small, dark, rubber-stoppered bottle. "I know this surgical nurse," he said almost apologetically.

"Let's go."

"I can do it. What's the dose?"

"I'm coming with you," Miles said.

"You are?"

"You think chiropractors can't give shots?"

"I think I'm looking at a chiropractor who's a brave man. All right. I'll be glad to have your help. You realize there's blood up there?"

"Of course. Let's go."

"No," John Shumaker said. "You're not going any-where until we call that Ranger."

"Fuck you, John," Joe said, going out the door. "You come along, and pick up Arnie. He's the one with the telephone."

They were outside now. Shumaker said: "Why do you have Carl's wagon?"

"Mr. Shumaker, prior to shooting my brother, your son let all the air out of my truck tires to try to keep me away from his little manhunt."

"He went crazy, Joe. He said your brother'd good as murdered him. He was sure of it."

"You can tell him different."

"You knew he was disturbed. You shouldn't have hurt him."

"I didn't, any more than I had to."

"I think it's a police matter, what you've done."

John Shumaker sure was thinking straight. "Really?" Joe said. "What's shooting people? A boy scout matter? I'll need the wagon. Bring your car."

At the turn-in for the bear trap John Shumaker stopped, got out and went to his son. Joe drove the wagon to the end of the road, where he and Miles got out and trotted into the woods together. Arnie was sitting on the log at Tommy's side.

Arnie stood up. "You got the stuff?"

"Yes. How's he doing?"

"Maybe resting easier but I'm glad you got the stuff."

Smiling weakly, Tommy nodded. "Oh, boy," he said.

Miles was already measuring some of the fluid into the cylinder of the hypodermic.

"Listen, Arnie," Joe said, "you'll find John Shumaker at the bear trap. Let him drive you to your telephone so he can call the Ranger for the key, okay?"

"You sure you want that boy turned loose?"

"We'll be gone by the time the Ranger gets here."

"Don't stop and say goodbye, Top. Once you're on the road, don't stop till you get to a hospital."

"Okay, Arnie." Joe hugged him. "Goodbye."

"Goodbye. Bye, Tommy. Doc, I'll see you, I guess." Arnie trotted off. The hypodermic was ready.

"Your bandage looks pretty good. Let's give him the shot."

"I'll do it," Joe said. "Where?"

"Either arm."

Joe undid Tommy's right cuff button and pushed up the sleeve.

"Nurses sure are getting ugly these days," Tommy said, and Joe gave him the shot. "How fast does it work?"

"Fast," said Doc Miles.

And in a few minutes Tommy said, "Oh, Jesus. Thank you. Oh man." The smile was pretty strong now.

"Okay," Joe said. "Now we're going to get you out of here."

"Don't try to carry me."

"I've carried the wounded before."

"Not this much wounded."

"No, you're probably right. Let's check for bleeding."

He loosened the tourniquet and watched the bandage. "Looks like it's stopped."

"That's the problem," Doc Miles said. "We could try making a seat with our hands but we don't want to start him bleeding again."

"If you wheel my cycle back I think I could crawl on and straddle it. You guys can balance me while I ride real slow."

"Our young friend shot the tires out, Tommy. It'd be a tough ride."

"Those were the first two shots, then," Tommy said.

"We'll rig something up," Joe said. "Want to give me a hand, Doc?"

"Sure," Doc Miles said.

"You'll be okay for a few more minutes, Tom?"

"As long as this beautiful stuff doesn't wear off."

19

Now HE knew that the first two shots had been his tires. He'd been half-asleep, trying rather blissfully to decide whether to drift off or have another drink first, dawdling, very comfortable in the sleeping bag, when he heard a car coming fast. Thought it might be the dear lads from Pennsylvania coming back, so he scuttled away and was in the woods when he heard the tire shots.

Then he started to run, not that he was much of a sprinter these days, and Crazy Shumaker saw him. Shot at him through the trees. Tommy still didn't know who it was. Heard the wagon coming up to the end of the road. Tommy was hiding by then, and when he saw Dippy Dipshit get out, Tommy stepped forth, showed mom's automatic, and said,

"Turn around and leave, friend."

"Fucking killer." Carl raised the rifle. Tommy took a shot at him, turned and ran some more. Carl shot, and came running after him.

They traded shots again, the little pistol going *snap* and the rifle saying *crack*.

Tommy ran again, almost laughing at how awkwardly he was moving. He stumbled over a log and fell forward, just as Looney Littleballs shot again. It was a freak hit, getting it in the ankle that way. He hitched himself around, saw Carl coming, saw him stop and rest his rifle barrel against a tree to take aim. He fired the last shot out of the pistol, and got down behind the log, hurting really bad, yelling about it, and then the next thing it was Carl yelling, and Tommy watched Joe take the kid.

Now he started thinking about Joe. And Little Joe. The two people he loved in this world. Wondering about staying in Joe's house as he got sicker. Not liking that much. How messy he'd be. Hating the idea of telling Little Joe. Feeling a lot of fear. A lot of it, and not just for when the painkiller would wear off.

20

THE MAUL Joe had used to dismount his tire was still leaning against a tree at site 17, just where he'd left it. Joe picked it up.

"What are you going to do with that?" Doc Miles asked.

"Hit myself over the head with it," Joe said. "No, I've got an idea."

He took the maul down to the bank where he and Arnie'd left the canoe. Miles followed.

"I'm about to manufacture a waterborne stretcher," Joe said, pulling the boat the rest of the way up on land. "Can you hold your side steady?"

"You're going to knock the center strut out?"

"Have to. My screwdrivers are across the river, in the truck. We'll cut up the foam pad for the bottom of the boat. We can turn the canoe on its side and roll Tommy into it, straighten it up and slide it on the ground over to the water. Then I can wade and tow it along, close to the bank, till we get to the place by site 14 where you can drive close to the water."

"It should work," Miles said. "Pound away." He knelt down across the boat from Joe and held the side.

For Joe, hitting the canoe was like smashing one of his fingers. "Sorry, old friend," he said as the strut came loose on his side, and he found he could break it away from the other side without pounding.

Cutting up the foam pad was a lot harder than he'd expected, but he got that done and asked Doc Miles to put on the waders and the gloves.

"I'd like you to have all the protection possible when we roll Tommy into this thing."

"They're your waders, Joe."

"If I'm exposed, I'm exposed," Joe said. "Put them on." Miles did.

He got Tommy's tent rope back out to use for a tow rope. They shoved the canoe into the back of the wagon, drove it up to the end of the road and slid it out.

"It's light," Doc Miles said. "Let's carry it."

Joe picked up the bow, Doc Miles the stern and they walked in that way until they came to the log.

"Jesus," Joe said. "It's the right log, isn't it?" It wasn't really a question. There was blood on it and around it. "Tommy," he shouted. "Tommy."

"He can't be gone," Doc Miles said.

"He could have dragged himself," Joe said. There was a trail of disturbed leaves on the forest floor. They followed it to the river. There was blood on an exposed rock three feet out in the water.

"Tommy," Joe yelled. "Tommy," and splashed out into the river, looking wildly downstream. There was nothing he could see downstream but water, and this time the tug of it against his legs was something fearful.

"Oh, God," he said, turned, splashed back. "God, Tommy."

Joe McKay slipped, fell to his knees on the riverbank, and wept.

Then he stood up and said, "I'm going back for a paddle. I'm going to take this canoe down the river."

"No, Joe," Doc Miles said, putting a hand on his arm. "No, there isn't any sense in that. Look at that water move."

Joe looked, and let Miles put an arm around his shoulder. There was nothing he could do. He knew the river. Nothing. "Come on. I'm going to leave the canoe, then."

"It can be repaired."

"It's old. Been through a lot. Let it rest in the woods. Come on. I'll drive you to your camp." Then he turned the canoe over, so it wouldn't fill with rain.

"Joe, I'm sure sorry."

"I know." This time it was Joe who put his arm around Doc Miles' shoulder, and they walked out of the woods together to the GMAC wagon.

The blue Oldsmobile was still parked alongside the road opposite site 17. John Shumaker was staying at the bear trap with his boy.

"I'll get off here," Doc Miles said, and Joe let him out.

He turned into 17 and parked beside the remains of his pop-up camper.

Ah-ha. Yeah. He closed his eyes. Opened them. Shit. Okay.

He'd load the wheels from Tommy's motorcycle, put them in the wagon. Then he'd drive across and collect the four wheels from his truck. He'd have to buy two tires and get four put back in shape in Millinockett. Then he'd have to come back to this frantic fucking place, get his truck going, leave the wagon, pick up the motorcycle and probably pull its trailer. He'd be ready to pack what little was left of his own stuff, and go home.

He'd stop, he guessed, at Little Joe's school on the way.

He went and sat at the picnic table for a while. The smoker and the radio were on it. He thought he'd leave them both for Arnie, call the old man from Millinocket, tell him to pick them up.

He went over to Tommy's trailer and opened it. Little Joe might want the Redneck Stradivarius. Little Joe could play some. They might give the clarinet to the school.

Joe took the bagpipe out of its case. He went back to the picnic table, put the pipe on it and looked at it a while, knowing what he was going to do.

He put the pipe together. He hadn't tried to play in years, but once he'd known "The Braes of Locheil," the slow song, the going-home song. He took the pipe and walked down to the river.

He'd probably get it wrong, here and there, but there weren't any music lovers around to tell him so, unless Mama Moose and Junior happened by.

He blew up the bag, tucked it under his arm and hit it to start the sound. The drone began, and he stood at attention, directing the music downstream, started the song and played it through. Then he waded into the river a few steps, set the bagpipe down in the water and watched the red-plaid bugger turn on its lazy side and float jauntily away, like some kind of goofy, Scotch, freshwater octopus, with half its legs sticking up in the air.

21

Uncle Joe could hardly ever score on him without fouling when they played one-on-one that summer, and they played pretty much every day.

They'd started as soon as he got here from school, and the score was about a thousand to forty-eight—he didn't bother keeping his own, but he secretly wrote down Uncle Joe's. The backboard was up over the garage door.

"Spend your time practicing. Get in shape for your basketball camp," Uncle Joe said the first day.

"Can't I work at the truck stop?"

"What can you do, Joker?"

Joker was his Connecticut name, now that he was too big to be called Little. "If you can't use me at the truck stop I'd like to get some other job, please."

"You don't exactly need the money."

"I don't like hanging loose."

"Okay. Let's get your rubber boots tomorrow and I'll put you in the truck wash. But you've still got to spend some time playing ball."

"Where's your ball? Come on."

You had to call your own fouls, and Uncle Joe was tough on himself about it. Generally it was charging. Uncle Joe had twenty pounds on Joker, and time and time again the old army ball player would slam in for a lay-up, bouncing a guy off the garage door.

"Good move, Uncle Joe," Joker would say.

"No. You were holding your ground. I fouled again."

Joker had this secret bet with himself that his uncle wouldn't get to a hundred before Joker left for camp. He liked working on defense, if you could call it work for a guy that had forty-three years on his uncle, three inches of height, longer arms and was never out of practice. He liked blocking shots best, better than scoring or rebounds, and the orthopedist who was team doctor at school said Joker would hit six-six, maybe seven, before he stopped growing.

Today they'd played a long time in the July heat, and Uncle Joe hadn't made one yet.

"Let's quit and get a beer, kiddo. Maybe it'll stunt your growth, and I'll have a chance in this game."

"Maybe I ought to run first."

"Did you this morning?"

"Three miles."

"That's enough in weather like this."

They went indoors, into the kitchen.

"Did you and Dad play one-on-one when you were kids?"

"Not much. Horse was his game. He was okay from the line."

"What was his shot like?"

"Kind of off-balance, from the chest, but it went in a lot." Uncle Joe opened the fridge and got out two cans of Amstel Light. "Last two. Need to get some more."

"I'd like to have seen that."

"Missing your Dad?"

"I never saw that much of him. Only in the last year or two—but I was starting to like him a lot. Sure I miss him. I wish he was here with us."

"So do I." Uncle Joe must have drunk practically his

whole can of beer first swallow. "You've got to call your Mom tonight."

"What's the time difference?"

"Six hours."

"He died a clean death, didn't he?"

"Yes."

"His life wasn't all that clean, though."

"Shut up, Joker. He had a lot of fun. He helped a lot of people. And people are going to be listening to his records for a while."

"And then they won't."

"Go take that run, mousebrain. Sweat that kind of crap out of yourself."

"You mean it?"

"Hell, yes."

"You going to run with me?"

"Hell, no. I'm going to sit here and finish your beer."

Joker felt like hugging him, so he did.